LUCY GAYHEART

BY

WILLA CATHER

LucyGayheart

VINTAGE BOOKS
A Division of Random House
New York

VINTAGE BOOKS EDITION, June 1976
Copyright 1935 by Willa Cather
Copyright renewed 1962 by Edith Lewis and the City Bank
Farmers Trust Co. All rights reserved under International
and Pan-American Copyright Conventions. Published in
the United States by Random House, Inc., New York, and
simultaneously in Canada by Random House of Canada
Limited, Toronto. Originally published by Alfred A.
Knopf, Inc., in August, 1935.

Library of Congress Cataloging in Publication Data
Cather, Willa Sibert, 1873–1947.
    Lucy Gayheart.

    I. Title.
PZ3.C2858Lu7 [PS3505.A87]   813'.5'2   75-28046
ISBN 0-394-71756-2
        Manufactured in the United States of America
                        3579B8642

Lucy Gayheart

BOOK I

BOOK I

I

In Haverford on the Platte the townspeople still talk of Lucy Gayheart. They do not talk of her a great deal, to be sure; life goes on and we live in the present. But when they do mention her name it is with a gentle glow in the face or the voice, a confidential glance which says: " Yes, you, too, remember? " They still see her as a slight figure always in motion; dancing or skating, or walking swiftly with intense direction, like a bird flying home.

When there is a heavy snowfall, the older people look out of their windows and remember how Lucy used to come darting through just such storms, her muff against her cheek, not shrinking, but giving her body to the wind as if she were catching step with it. And in the heat of summer she came just as swiftly down the long shaded side-walks and across the open squares blistering in the sun. In the breathless glare of August noons, when the horses hung their heads and the work-men " took it slow," she never took it slow. Cold, she used to say, made her feel more alive; heat must have had the same effect.

The Gayhearts lived at the west edge of Haver-ford, half a mile from Main Street. People said " out to the Gayhearts' " and thought it rather a long walk in summer. But Lucy covered the dis-tance a dozen times a day, covered it quickly with that walk so peculiarly her own, like an expression of irrepressible light-heartedness. When the old women at work in their gardens caught sight of her in the distance, a mere white figure under the flickering shade of the early summer trees, they always knew her by the way she moved. On she came, past hedges and lilac bushes and woolly-green grape arbours and rows of jonquils, and one knew she was delighted with everything; with her summer clothes and the air and the sun and the blossoming world. There was something in her nature that was like her movements, something direct and unhesitating and joyous, and in her golden-brown eyes. They were not gentle brown eyes, but flashed with gold sparks like that Colo-rado stone we call the tiger-eye. Her skin was rather dark, and the colour in her lips and cheeks was like the red of dark peonies — deep, velvety. Her mouth was so warm and impulsive that every shadow of feeling made a change in it.

Photographs of Lucy mean nothing to her old friends. It was her gaiety and grace they loved. Life seemed to lie very near the surface in her. She had that singular brightness of young beauty: flower gardens have it for the first few hours after sunrise.

We missed Lucy in Haverford when she went away to Chicago to study music. She was eighteen years old then; talented, but too careless and light-hearted to take herself very seriously. She never dreamed of a " career." She thought of music as a natural form of pleasure, and as a means of earning money to help her father when she came home. Her father, Jacob Gayheart, led the town band and gave lessons on the clarinet, flute, and violin, at the back of his watch-repairing shop. Lucy had given piano lessons to beginners ever since she was in the tenth grade. Children liked her, because she never treated them like children; they tried to please her, especially the little boys.

Though Jacob Gayheart was a good watchmaker, he wasn't a good manager. Born of Bavarian parents in the German colony at Belleville,

Illinois, he had learned his trade under his father. He came to Haverford young and married an American wife, who brought him a half-section of good farm land. After her death he borrowed money on this farm to buy another, and now they were both mortgaged. That troubled his older daughter, Pauline, but it did not trouble Mr. Gayheart. He took more pains to make the band boys practise than he did to keep up his interest payments. He was a town character, of course, and people joked about him, though they were proud of their band. Mr. Gayheart looked like an old daguerreotype of a minor German poet; he wore a moustache and goatee and had a fine sweep of dark hair above his forehead, just a little grey at the sides. His intelligent, lazy hazel eyes seemed to say: " But it's a very pleasant world, why bother? "

He managed to enjoy every day from start to finish. He got up early in the morning and worked for an hour in his flower garden. Then he took his bath and dressed for the day, selecting his shirt and necktie as carefully as if he were going to pay a visit. After breakfast he lit a good cigar and walked into town, never missing the flavour of his tobacco for a moment. Usually he put a flower in his coat before he left home. No one ever got more satisfaction out of good health and simple pleasures and a blue-and-gold band uniform than Jacob Gayheart. He was probably the happiest man in Haverford.

2

It was the end of the Christmas holidays, the Christmas of 1901, Lucy's third winter in Chicago. She was spending her vacation at home. There had been good skating all through Christmas week, and she had made the most of it. Even on her last afternoon, when she should have been packing, she was out with a party of Haverford boys and girls, skating on the long stretch of ice north of Duck Island. This island, nearly half a mile in length, split the river in two, — or, rather, it split a shallow arm off the river. The Platte River proper was on the south side of this island and it seldom froze over; but the shallow stream between the island and the north shore froze deep and made smooth ice. This was before the days of irrigation from the Platte; it was then a formidable river in flood time. During the spring freshets it sometimes cut out a new channel in the soft farm land along its banks and changed its bed altogether.

At about four o'clock on this December afternoon a light sleigh with bells and buffalo robes and a good horse came rapidly along the road from town and turned at Benson's corner into the skating-place. A tall young man sprang out, tied his horse to the hitch-bar, where a row of sleighs already stood, and hurried to the shore with his skating-shoes in his hand. As he put them on, he scanned the company moving over the ice. It was not hard to pick out the figure he was looking for. Six of the strongest skaters had left the others behind and were going against the wind, toward the end of the island. Two were in advance of the rest, Jim Hardwick and Lucy Gayheart. He knew her by her brown squirrel jacket and fur cap, and by her easy stroke. The two ends of a long crimson scarf were floating on the wind behind her, like two slender crimson wings.

Harry Gordon struck out across the ice to over- take her. He, too, was a fine skater; a big fellow, the heavy-weight boxer type, and as light on his feet as a boxer. Nevertheless he was a trifle winded when he passed the group of four and shot along- side Jim Hardwick.

"Jim," he called, "will you give me a turn with Lucy before the sun goes down?"

"Sure, Harry. I was only keeping her out of mischief for you." The lad fell back. Haverford boys gave way to Harry Gordon good-naturedly.

Book I

He was the rich young man of the town, and he was not arrogant or overbearing. He was known as a good fellow; rather hard in business, but liberal with the ball team and the band; public-spirited, people said.

"Why, Harry, you said you weren't coming!" Lucy exclaimed as she took his arm.

"Didn't think I could. I did, though. Drove Flicker into a lather getting out here after the directors' meeting. This is the best part of the afternoon, anyway. Come along." They crossed hands and went straight ahead in two-step time.

The sun was dropping low in the south, and all the flat snow-covered country, as far as the eye could see, was beginning to glow with a rose-coloured light, which presently would deepen to orange and flame. The black tangle of willows on the island made a thicket like a thorn hedge, and the knotty, twisted, slow-growing scrub-oaks with flat tops took on a bronze glimmer in that intense oblique light which seemed to be setting them on fire.

As the sun declined, the wind grew sharper. They had left the skating party far behind. "Shan't we turn?" Lucy gasped presently.

"Not yet. I want to get into that sheltered fork of the island. I have some Scotch whisky in my pocket; that will warm you up."

" How nice! I'm getting a little tired. I've been out a long while."

The end of the island forked like a fish's tail. When they had rounded one of these points, Harry swung her in to the shore. They sat down on a bleached cottonwood log, where the black willow thicket behind them made a screen. The interlacing twigs threw off red light like incandescent wires, and the snow underneath was rose-colour. Harry poured Lucy some whisky in the metal cup that screwed over the stopper; he himself drank from the flask. The round red sun was falling like a heavy weight; it touched the horizon line and sent quivering fans of red and gold over the wide country. For a moment Lucy and Harry Gordon were sitting in a stream of blinding light; it burned on their skates and on the flask and the metal cup. Their faces became so brilliant that they looked at each other and laughed. In an instant the light was gone; the frozen stream and the snow-masked prairie land became violet, under the blue-green sky. Wherever one looked there was nothing but flat country and low hills, all violet and grey. Lucy gave a long sigh.

Gordon lifted her from the log and they started back, with the wind behind them. They found the river empty, a lonely stretch of blue-grey ice; all the skaters had gone. Harry knew by her stroke that Lucy was tired. She had been out a long while before he came, and she had made a special effort to skate with him. He was sorry and pleased. He guided her in to the shore at some distance from his sleigh, knelt down and took off her skating shoes, changed his own, and with a sudden movement swung her up in his arms and carried her over the trampled snow to his cutter. As he tucked her under the buffalo robes she thanked him.

" The wind seems to have made me very sleepy, Harry. I'm afraid I won't do much packing tonight. No matter; there's tomorrow. And it was a good skate."

On the drive home Gordon let his sleigh-bells (very musical bells, he had got them to please Lucy) do most of the talking. He knew when to be quiet.

Lucy felt drowsy and dreamy, glad to be warm. The sleigh was such a tiny moving spot on that still white country settling into shadow and silence. Suddenly Lucy started and struggled under the tight blankets. In the darkening sky she had seen the first star come out; it brought her heart into her throat. That point of silver light spoke to her like a signal, released another kind of life and feeling which did not belong here. It over-powered her. With a mere thought she had reached that star and it had answered, recognition had flashed between. Something knew, then, in the unknowing waste: something had always known, forever! That joy of saluting what is far above one was an eternal thing, not merely something that had happened to her ignorance and her foolish heart.

The flash of understanding lasted but a moment. Then everything was confused again. Lucy shut her eyes and leaned on Harry's shoulder to escape from what she had gone so far to snatch. It was too bright and too sharp. It hurt, and made one feel small and lost.

3

The following night, Sunday evening, all the boys and girls who had been at home for the vacation were going back to school. Most of them would stop at Lincoln; Lucy was the only one going through to Chicago. The train from the west was due to leave Haverford at seven-thirty, and by seven o'clock sleighs and wagons from all directions were driving toward the railway station at the south end of town.

The station platform was soon full of restless young people, glancing up the track, looking at their watches, as if they could not endure their own town a moment longer. Presently a carriage drawn by two horses dashed up to the siding, and the swaying crowd ran to meet it, shouting.

" Here she is, here's Fairy! "

" Fairy Blair! "

" Hello, Fairy! "

Out jumped a yellow-haired girl, supple and quick as a kitten, with a little green Tyrolese hat pulled tight over her curls. She ripped off her grey fur coat, threw it into the air for the boys to catch, and ran down the platform in her travelling suit — a black velvet jacket and scarlet waistcoat, with a skirt very short indeed for the fashion of that time. Just then a man came out from the station and called that the train would be twenty minutes late. Groans and howls broke from the crowd.

" Oh, hell! "

" What in thunder can we do? "

The green hat shrugged and laughed. " Shut up. Quit swearing. We'll wake the town."

She caught two boys by the elbow, and between these stiffly overcoated figures raced out into the silent street, swaying from left to right, pushing the boys as if she were shaking two saplings, and doing an occasional shuffle with her feet. She had a pretty, common little face, and her eyes were so lit-up and reckless that one might have thought she had been drinking. Her fresh little mouth, without being ugly, was really very naughty. She couldn't push the boys fast enough; suddenly she sprang from between the two rigid figures as if she had been snapped out of a sling-shot and ran up the street with the whole troop at her heels. They were all a little crazy, but as she was the craziest, they followed her. They swerved aside to let the town bus pass.

The bus backed up to the siding. Mr. Gayheart alighted and gave a hand to each of his daughters. Pauline, the elder, got out first. She was short and stout and blonde, like the Prestons, her mother's people. She was twelve years Lucy's senior. (Two boys, born between the daughters, died in childhood.) It was Pauline who had brought her sister up; their mother died when Lucy was only six.

Pauline was talking as she got out of the bus, urging her father to hurry and get the trunk checked. " There are always a lot of people in the baggage room, and it takes Bert forever to check a trunk. And be sure you tell him to get it onto this train. When Mrs. Young went to Minneapolis her trunk lay here for twenty-four hours after she started, and she didn't get it until . . ." But Mr. Gayheart walked calmly away and lost the story of Mrs. Young's trunk. Lucy remained standing beside her sister, but she did not hear it either. She was thinking of something else.

Pauline took Lucy's arm determinedly, as if it were the right thing to do, and for a moment she was silent. "Look, there's Harry Gordon's sleigh coming up, with the Jenks boy driving. Do you suppose he is going east tonight?"

"He said he might go to Omaha," Lucy replied carelessly.

"That's nice. You will have company," said Pauline, with the rough-and-ready heartiness she often used to conceal annoyance.

Lucy made no comment, but looked in through a window at the station clock. She had never wanted so much to be moving; to be alone and to feel the train gliding along the smooth rails; to watch the little stations flash by.

Fairy Blair, in her Tyrolese hat, came back from her run quite out of breath and supported by the two boys. As she passed the Gayheart sisters she called:

"Off for the East, Lucy? Wish I were going with you. You musical people get all the fun." As she and her overcoated props came to a standstill she watched Lucy out of the tail of her eye. They were the two most popular girls in Haverford, and Fairy found Lucy frightfully stuffy and girly-girly. Whenever she met Harry Gordon she tossed her head and flashed at him a look which plainly said: " What in hell do you want with *that?* "

Mr. Gayheart returned, gave his daughter her trunk check, and stood looking up at the sky. Among other impractical pursuits he had studied astronomy from time to time. When at last the scream of the whistle shivered through the still winter air, Lucy drew a quick breath and started forward. Her father took her arm and pressed it softly; it was not wise to show too much affection for his younger daughter. A long line of swaying lights came out of the flat country to the west, and a moment later the white beam from the headlight streamed along the steel rails at their feet. The great locomotive, coated with hoar-frost, passed them and stopped, panting heavily.

Pauline snatched her sister and gave her a clumsy kiss. Mr. Gayheart picked up Lucy's bag and led the way to the right car. He found her seat, arranged her things neatly, then stood looking at her with a discerning, appreciative smile. He liked pretty girls, even in his own family. He put his arm around her, and as he kissed her he murmured in her ear: " She's a nice girl, my Lucy! " Then he went slowly down the car and got off just as the porter was taking up the step. Pauline was already in a fret, convinced that he would be carried on to the next station.

In Lucy's car were several boys going back to the University at Lincoln. They at once came to her seat and began talking to her. When Harry Gordon entered and walked down the aisle, they drew back, but he shook his head.

" I'm going out to the diner now. I'll be back later."

Lucy shrugged as he passed on. Wasn't that just like him? Of course he knew that she, and all the other students, would have eaten an early supper at the family board before they started; but he might have asked her and the boys to go out to the dining-car with him and have a dessert or a Welsh rabbit. Another instance of the instinctive unwastefulness which had made the Gordons rich! Harry could be splendidly extravagant upon occasion, but he made an occasion of it; it was the outcome of careful forethought.

Lucy gave her whole attention to the lads who were so pleased to have it. They were all about her own age, while Harry was eight years older. Fairy Blair was holding a little court at the other end of the car, but distance did not muffle her occasional spasmodic laugh — a curious laugh, like a bleat, which had the effect of an indecent gesture. When this mirth broke out, the boys who were beside Lucy looked annoyed, and drew closer to her, as if protesting their loyalty. She was sorry when Harry Gordon came back and they went away. She received him rather coolly, but he didn't notice that at all. He began talking at once about the new street-lamps they were to have in Haverford; he and his father had borne half the cost of them.

Harry sat comfortably back in the Pullman seat, but he did not lounge. He sat like a gentleman. He had a good physical presence, whether in action or repose. He was immensely conceited, but not nervously or aggressively so. Instead of being a weakness in him, it amounted to a kind of strength. Such easy self-possession was very reassuring to a mercurial, vacillating person like Lucy.

Tonight, as it happened, Lucy wanted to be alone; but ordinarily she was glad to meet Harry anywhere; to pass him in the post-office or to see him coming down the street. If she stopped for only a word with him, his vitality and unfailing satisfaction with life set her up. No matter what they talked about, it was amusing. She felt absolutely free with him, and she found everything about him genial; his voice, his keen blue eyes, his fresh skin and sandy hair. People said he was hard in business and took advantage of borrowers in a tight place; but neither his person nor his manner gave a hint of such qualities.

While he was chatting confidentially with her about the new street-lamps, Harry noticed that Lucy's hands were restless and that she moved about in her seat.

"What's the matter, Lucy? You're fidgety."

She pulled herself up and smiled. "Isn't it silly! Travelling always makes me nervous. But I'm not very used to it, you know."

"You're in a hurry to get back. I can tell," he nodded knowingly. "How about the opera this spring? Will you let me come on for a week and go with me every night?"

"Oh, that will be splendid! But I don't know about every night. I'm teaching now, you see. I'm much busier than I was last year."

"We can fix that all right. I'll make a call on Auerbach. I got on with him first-rate. I told him I had known you ever since you were a youngster." Harry chuckled and leaned forward a little. "Do you know the first time I ever saw you, Lucy? It was in the old skating-rink. I suppose Haverford was about the last town on earth to have a skating-rink."

"But that was ages ago. The old rink was pulled down before your bank was built."

"That's right. Father and I were staying at the hotel. We had come on to look the town over. One afternoon I was passing the rink and I heard a piano going, so I went in. An old man was playing a waltz, *Hearts and Flowers* I think they called it. There were a bunch of people on the floor, but I picked you out first shot. You must have been about thirteen, with your hair down your back. You had on a short skirt and a skin-tight red jersey, and you were going like a streak. I thought you had the prettiest eyes in the world — Still think so," he added, puckering his brows, as if he were making a grave admission.

Lucy laughed. Harry was cautious, even in compliments.

"Oh, thank you, Harry! I had such good times in that old rink. I missed it terribly after it was pulled down. Pauline wouldn't let me go to dances then. But I don't remember you very well until you began to pitch for Haverford. Everyone was crazy about your in-curves. Why did you give up baseball?"

"Too lazy, I guess." He shrugged his smooth shoulders. "I liked playing ball, though. But now about the opera. You'll keep the first two weeks of April open for me? I can't tell now just when I'll be able to run on."

Young Gordon was watching Lucy as they talked, and thinking that he had about made up his mind. He wasn't rash, he hadn't been in a hurry. He didn't like the idea of marrying the watch-

maker's daughter, when so many brilliant oppor-
tunities were open to him. But as he had often told
himself before, he would just have to swallow
the watchmaker. During the two winters Lucy
had been away in Chicago, he had played about
with lots of girls in the cities where his father's
business took him. But there was simply nobody
like her, — for him, at least.

Tomorrow he would have to deal with a
rather delicate situation. Harriet Arkwright, of
the St. Joseph Arkwrights, was visiting a friend
in Omaha, and she had telephoned him to come on
and take her to a dance. He had carried things
along pretty far with Miss Arkwright. Her favour
was flattering to a small-town man. She was a person of position in St. Joe. Her father was president of the oldest banking house, and she had a
considerable fortune of her own, from her mother.
If she was twenty-six years old and still unmar-
ried, it was not from lack of suitors. She had been
in no hurry to tie herself up. She managed her
own property very successfully, travelled a good
deal, liked her independence. A woman of the
world, Harry considered her; good style, always
at her ease, had a kind of authority that money
and social position give. But she was plain, con-
found it! She looked like the men of her family.
And she had a hard, matter-of-fact voice, which

never kindled with anything; slightly nasal. Whatever she spoke of, she divested of charm. If she thanked him for his gorgeous roses, her tone deflowered the flowers.

Harry liked to play with the idea of how such a marriage would affect his future, but he had never tried to make himself believe that he was in love with Harriet. Strangely enough, the only girl who gave him any deep thrill was this same Lucy, who lived in his own town, was poor as a church mouse, never flattered him, and often laughed at him. When he was with her, life was different; that was all.

And she was growing up, he realized. All through the Christmas vacation he had felt a change in her. She was perhaps a trifle more reserved. At the dance, on New Year's Eve, he thought she held herself away from him just a little — and from everyone else. She wasn't cold, she had never looked lovelier, never been more playfully affectionate toward her old friends. But she was not there in the old way. All evening her eyes shone with something she did not tell him. The moment she was not talking to someone, that look came back. And in every waltz she seemed to be looking over his shoulder at something — positively enchanting! . . . whereas there was only the same old crowd, dancing in the Masonic Hall, with a " crash " over the Masonic carpet. He would not soon forget that New Year's Eve. It had brought him up short. Lucy wasn't an artless, happy little country girl any longer; she was headed toward something. He had better be making up his mind. Even tonight, here on the train, when she seemed to give him her whole attention, she didn't, really.

The porter came for Gordon's bags, and said they were pulling into Omaha. Lucy went out to the vestibule with Harry, and they talked in low tones during the stop. He stood holding her hand and looking down at her with that blue-eyed friendliness which seemed so transparent and uncalculating, until the porter called " All aboard! " Harry kissed her on the cheek and stepped down to the station platform. Lucy waved to him through the window while the train was pulling out.

Gordon got into a horse cab and started for his hotel. His chin was lowered in his muffler, and he smiled at the street-lights as the cab rattled along. Yes, he told himself, he must use diplomacy with Miss Arkwright for a while longer. Her stock was going down. He meant to commit the supreme extravagance and marry for beauty. He meant to have a wife other men would envy him.

Lucy undressed quickly, got into her berth, and turned off the lights. At last she was alone, lying

still in the dark, and could give herself up to the
vibration of the train, — a rhythm that had to
do with escape, change, chance, with life hurrying
forward. That sense of release and surrender
went all over her body; she seemed to lie in it
as in a warm bath. Tomorrow night at this time
she would be coming home from Clement Sebastian's recital. In a few hours one could cover that
incalculable distance; from the winter country and
homely neighbours, to the city where the air
trembled like a tuning-fork with unimaginable
possibilities.

Lucy carried in her mind a very individual map
of Chicago: a blur of smoke and wind and noise,
with flashes of blue water, and certain clear out-
lines rising from the confusion; a high building
on Michigan Avenue where Sebastian had his
studio — the stretch of park where he sometimes
walked in the afternoon — the Cathedral door out
of which she had seen him come one morning —
the concert hall where she first heard him sing.
This city of feeling rose out of the city of fact like
a definite composition, — beautiful because the
rest was blotted out. She thought of the steps leading down from the Art Museum as perpetually
flooded with orange-red sunlight; they had been
like that one stormy November afternoon when
Sebastian came out of the building at five o'clock

and stopped beside one of the bronze lions to turn up the collar of his overcoat, light a cigarette, and look vaguely up and down the avenue before he hailed a cab and drove away.

In the round of her day's engagements, hurrying about Chicago from one place to another, Lucy often came upon spots which gave her a sudden lift of the heart, made her feel glad before she knew why. Tonight, lying in her berth, she thought she would be happy to be going back, even if Clement Sebastian were no longer there. She would still be going back to "the city," to the place where so many memories and sensations were piled up, where a window or a doorway or a street-corner with a magical meaning might at any moment flash out of the fog.

4

The next morning Lucy was in Chicago, in her own room, unpacking and putting her things to rights. She lived in a somewhat unusual manner; had a room two flights up over a bakery, in one of the grimy streets off the river.

When she first came to Chicago she had stayed at a students' boarding-house, but she didn't like the pervasive informality of the place, nor the

Southern gentlewoman of fallen fortunes who
conducted it. She told her teacher, Professor Auerbach, that she would never get on unless she could
live alone with her piano, where there would be
no gay voices in the hall or friendly taps at her
door. Auerbach took her out to his house, and they
consulted with his wife. Mrs. Auerbach knew exactly what to do. She and Lucy went to see Mrs.
Schneff and her bakery.

The Schneff bakery was an old German land-
mark in that part of the city. On the ground floor
was the bake shop, and a homely restaurant spe-
cializing in German dishes, conducted by Mrs.
Schneff. On the top floor was a glove factory. The
three floors between, the Schneffs rented to people
who did not want to take long leases; travelling
salesmen, clerks, railroad men who must be near
the station. The food in the bakery downstairs
was good enough, and there were no table companions or table jokes. Everyone had his own
little table, attended to his own business, and read
his paper. Lucy had taken a room here at once,
and for the first time in her life she could come and
go like a boy; no one fussing about, no one hover-
ing over her. There were inconveniences, to be
sure. The lodgers came and went by an open stairway which led up from the street beside the front

door of the restaurant; the winter winds blew up through the halls — burglars might come, too, but so far they never had. There was no parlour in which Lucy could receive callers. When she went anywhere with one of Auerbach's students, the young man waited for her on the stairway, or met her in the restaurant below.

This morning Lucy was glad as never before to be back with her own things and her own will. After she had unpacked, she arranged and re-arranged; nothing was too much trouble. The moment she had shut the door upon the baggage man, she seemed to find herself again. Out there in Haverford she had scarcely been herself at all; she had been trying to feel and behave like some-one she no longer was; as children go on playing the old games to please their elders, after they have ceased to be children at heart. Coming up from the station, through a pecking fall of sleet, she wondered whether something she had left in this room might have vanished in her absence; might not be there to welcome her. It was here she had come the night after she first heard Clement Sebastian, and here she had brought back all her chance glimpses of him. These four walls held all her thoughts and feelings about him. Her mem-ories did not stand out separately; they were blended and pervasive. They made the room seem larger than it was, quieter and more guarded; gave it a slight austerity.

Since she was going to Sebastian's recital to-night, Lucy had her dinner early, in the restaurant below. When she came upstairs again, it was not yet time to dress. She put on her dressing-gown, turned out the gas light, and lay down to reflect.

Only three months ago, early in October, Professor Auerbach had told her that his old friend, Clement Sebastian, was in Chicago, and that she must hear him — probably he would not be there long. He was a man one couldn't afford to miss. But Lucy had little money and many wants; a baritone voice didn't seem to be one of the most vehement. She missed his first recital without regret, though afterwards the newspaper notices, and the talk she heard among the students, aroused her curiosity. The following week he gave a benefit recital for the survivors of a mine disaster. Auerbach got a single ticket for her, and she went alone. She had dressed here, in this room, without much enthusiasm, rather reluctant to go out again after a tiring day. She had turned on the steam heat and put out the gas and gone down-stairs, anticipating nothing.

Sebastian's personality had aroused her, even

before he began to sing, the moment he came upon
the stage. He was not young, was middle-aged,
indeed, with a stern face and large, rather tired
eyes. He was a very big man; tall, heavy, broad-
shouldered. He took up a great deal of space and
filled it solidly. His torso, sheathed in black broad-
cloth and a white waistcoat, was unquestionably
oval, but it seemed the right shape for him. She
said to herself immediately: " Yes, a great artist
should look like that."

The first number was a Schubert song she had
never heard or even seen. His diction was one of
the remarkable things about Sebastian's singing,
and she did not miss a word of the German. A
Greek sailor, returned from a voyage, stands in the
temple of Castor and Pollux, the mariners' stars,
and acknowledges their protection. He has steered
his little boat by their mild, protecting light, *eure
Milde, eure Wachen.* In recognition of their aid
he hangs his oar as a votive offering in the porch
of their temple.

The song was sung as a religious observance
in the classical spirit, a rite more than a prayer;
a noble salutation to beings so exalted that in the
mariner's invocation there was no humbleness and
no entreaty. *In your light I stand without fear, O
august stars! I salute your eternity.* That was the
feeling. Lucy had never heard anything sung with

such elevation of style. In its calmness and seren-
ity there was a kind of large enlightenment, like
daybreak.

After this invocation came five more Schubert
songs, all melancholy. They made Lucy feel that
there was something profoundly tragic about this
man. The dark beauty of the songs seemed to her a
quality in the voice itself, as kindness can be in the
touch of a hand. It was as simple as that — like
light changing on the water. When he began *Der
Doppelgänger,* the last song of the group (*Still
ist die Nacht, es ruhen die Gassen*), it was like
moonlight pouring down on the narrow street of
an old German town. With every phrase that picture deepened — moonlight, intense and calm,
sleeping on old human houses; and somewhere a
lonely black cloud in the night sky. *So manche
Nacht in alter Zeit?* The moon was gone, and the
silent street. — And Sebastian was gone, though
Lucy had not been aware of his exit. The black
cloud that had passed over the moon and the song
had obliterated him, too. There was nobody left
before the grey velvet curtain but the red-haired
accompanist, a lame boy, who dragged one foot
as he went across the stage.

Through the rest of the recital her attention
was intermittent. Sometimes she listened intently,
and the next moment her mind was far away. She

was struggling with something she had never felt before. A new conception of art? It came closer than that. A new kind of personality? But it was much more. It was a discovery about life, a revelation of love as a tragic force, not a melting mood, of passion that drowns like black water. As she sat listening to this man the outside world seemed to her dark and terrifying, full of fears and dangers that had never come close to her until now.

A note on the program said there would be no encores. After the last number, when the singer had repeatedly come back to acknowledge applause, the lights above the stage were turned out. But the audience remained seated. A French basso from the New York opera, who happened to be in town, occupied a stage box with a party of friends. He kept calling:

" Clément! Clément! "

At last the baritone came back, his coat on his arm and his hat in his hand. He bowed to his colleague, the bass, then turned aside and spoke through the stage door. The lame boy appeared; they had a word together under the applause. Sebastian walked to the front of the stage in the half-darkness and began to sing an old setting of Byron's *When We Two Parted;* a sad, simple old air which required little from the singer, yet probably no one who heard it that night will ever forget it.

Lucy had come home and up the stairs, into this room, tired and frightened, with a feeling that some protecting barrier was gone — a window had been broken that let in the cold and darkness of the night. Sitting here in her cloak, shivering, she had whispered over and over the words of that last song:

> When we two parted,
>   In silence and tears,
> Half broken-hearted,
>   To sever for years,
>
> Pale grew thy cheek and cold,
>   Colder thy kiss;
> Surely that hour foretold
>   Sorrow to this.

It was as if that song were to have some effect upon her own life. She tried to forget it, but it was unescapable. It was with her, like an evil omen; she could not get it out of her mind. For weeks afterwards it kept singing itself over in her brain. Her forebodings on that first night had not been mistaken; Sebastian had already destroyed a great deal for her. Some peoples' lives are affected by what happens to their person or their property; but for others fate is what happens to their feelings and their thoughts — that and nothing more.

Book I

The following day Lucy had questioned Paul Auerbach about Sebastian, at first timidly, then fiercely. What was his history? What had he been like as a boy? What made him different from other singers?

"Oh, but," said Professor Auerbach calmly, "Clement is very exceptional; he is a fine artist." This exasperated her. It was like saying, This is a black horse, or, This is a tall tree. Auerbach promised her that she should meet him some time, but it never seemed to come off.

Then one afternoon, a few days before the Christmas vacation, Auerbach came into the back room where Lucy was just finishing with a pupil and told her he had a surprise for her. Sebastian would be here at the studio at ten o'clock tomorrow morning. His accompanist, James Mockford, was to have an operation on his hip when he got home to England, and for the present his doctor wanted him to spend his mornings in bed. He might be able to keep his concert dates, if he got rid of the routine work. Sebastian was looking for someone to accompany him in his practice hours. He was coming tomorrow to try out several of Auerbach's pupils, and Lucy would have a chance to play for him.

"He wants someone young and teachable, not somebody who will try to teach him. I think you might please him, Lucy. I spoke for you."

That night, of course, she slept very little. She had never been nervous when Auerbach asked her to play for his friends; he had told her this was because she was not ambitious, — that it was her greatest fault. But this time it was different. If she didn't please Sebastian, she would probably never meet him again. If she did please him — But that possibility frightened her more than the other. For an ordinary singer she thought she could do very well; but she could never play for him. She hadn't it in her. By five o'clock in the morning she had decided not to appear at the studio at all; she would decline the risk.

With her breakfast, courage revived. To this day she could not remember how she ever got to Auerbach's studio, but she arrived there. As she approached the door, she heard Sebastian singing the *"Largo al Factotum"* from the *Barber of Seville*. It must be John Patterson at the piano. She slipped in quietly. It was an easier entrance than she had hoped for. When the aria was over, Auerbach introduced her. Sebastian was easy and kindly. He took her hand and looked straight into her eyes.

"Shall we set to work at once, Miss Gayheart, or had you rather wait a bit, while Mr. Schneller and I try our luck?"

" I'd rather try now, if you please," she said decidedly.

He laughed. " And get it over with? Don't be nervous. It's no great matter. We might try this same aria. I seemed not to do it very well."

Poor young Patterson flushed under his sandy hair; he knew what that meant.

" Have you ever played the piano accompaniment?" Sebastian asked as she sat down.

" I haven't happened to. But I've heard the opera."

When they finished he began turning over his music. " Now suppose we take something quite different." He put an aria from Massenet's *Hérodiade*, *"Vision fugitive,"* on the rack before her.

Afterwards he called Mr. Schneller, and Lucy sat in a deep corner of the sofa, remembering the mistakes she had made. Presently she heard Sebastian thanking the two young men and telling Auerbach they were a credit to him.

" Now, my boys, I won't keep you any longer. We will have another practice morning one of these days. I'm going to detain Miss Gayheart; she was a little nervous and I want her to try again." He shook hands with Schneller and Patterson, and they left. Then he took Auerbach's arm and walked with him toward the sofa where Lucy was sitting. " On the whole, Paul, I think

Miss Gayheart would be the best risk. She is a little uncertain, but she has much the best touch."

Auerbach spoke up for her.

" She's not usually uncertain. I was surprised when she went wrong in the Massenet. She reads well at sight."

" I was frightened, Mr. Auerbach," Lucy said feebly.

The large man in the double-breasted morning coat stood before her and smiled encouragingly. " I know when people are frightened, my dear. I've seen it before. The point is, you do not make ugly sounds; that puts me out more than anything. After the holidays you must come to my studio and we'll try an hour's practice together. That's the only way to arrive at anything. Just when do you get back from your vacation? "

On the 3rd of January, she told him.

"Very well, shall we say January 4th, at ten o'clock, in my studio on Michigan Avenue? " He took a notebook from his pocket and wrote it down. " You might take the score of *Elijah* with you and glance over it." Again he looked at her intently, with real kindness in his eyes. " Good-bye, Miss Gayheart, and a pleasant holiday."

That was the last time she had seen him.

Tonight she would hear his Schubert program, and tomorrow morning at ten she was to be at his studio.

Book I

* * *

Lucy sprang up from her bed; it was almost time to start for the concert. She slipped into her only evening dress and put on the velvet cloak she had bought just before she went home for Christmas. It was very pretty, she thought, and becoming (she had quite impoverished herself to have it), but it was not very warm. Tonight there was a bitter wind blowing off the Lake, but she was going to have a cab — anyway, she was not afraid of the cold. She rather liked the excitement of winding a soft, light cloak about her bare arms and shoulders and running out into a glacial cold through which one could hear the hammer-strokes of the workmen who were thawing out switches down on the freight tracks with gasoline torches. The thing to do was to make an overcoat of the cold; to feel one's self warm and awake at the heart of it, one's blood coursing unchilled in an air where roses froze instantly.

5

The recital this evening was given in a small hall, before an audience made up of Germans and Jews. Lucy arrived very early and was able to change her seat (which was near Auerbach's) for

one at the back of the house, in the shadow of a
pillar, where she could feel very much alone. She
had never heard *Die Winterreise* sung straight
through as an integral work. For her it was being
sung the first time, something newly created, and
she attributed to the artist much that belonged to
the composer. She kept feeling that this was not
an interpretation, this was the thing itself, with
one man and one nature behind every song.
The singing was not dramatic, in any way she
knew. Sebastian did not identify himself with this
melancholy youth; he presented him as if he were
a memory, not to be brought too near into the
present. One felt a long distance between the
singer and the scenes he was recalling, a long
perspective.

This evening Lucy tried to give some attention
to the accompanist — there was good reason,
surely, if she were to attempt to take his place tomorrow! Even at the other concert she had felt
that she had never heard anyone play for the voice
so well. *Die Krähe, Der Wegweiser* . . . there
was something uncanny in that young man's short,
insinuating fingers. She admired him, but she didn't
like him. Was she jealous, already? No, something
in his physical personality set her on edge a little.
He was picturesque — too picturesque. He had
the very white skin that sometimes goes with red

hair, and tonight, as he sat against an olive-green velvet curtain, his features seemed to disappear altogether. His face looked like a handful of flour thrown against the velvet. His head was rather flat behind the ears, and his red hair seemed to clasp it in a wreath of curls that were stiff but not tight. She thought she remembered plaster casts in the Art Museum with just such curls. For some reason she didn't like the way he moved across the stage. His lameness gave him a weak, undulating walk, "like a rag walking," she thought. It was contemptible to hold a man's infirmity against him; besides, if this young man weren't lame, she would not be going to Sebastian's studio tomorrow, — she would never have met him at all. How strange it was that James Mockford's bad hip should bring about the most important thing that had ever happened to her!

After the concert Paul Auerbach, in his old-fashioned dress coat and white lawn tie, came up to her. " I am going back to the artists' room, Lucy. Would you like to go with me? "

She hesitated. " No, thank you, Mr. Auerbach. I'd rather not. Will he really expect me tomorrow, do you think? "

6

The next morning Lucy was walking across the city toward Michigan Avenue. She was happy, she was frightened, — couldn't keep her attention on anything. Her mind had got away from her and was darting about in the sunlight, over the tops of the tall buildings. Exactly at ten o'clock she went into the Arts Building and told the hall porter she had an engagement with Mr. Sebastian. He rang for the elevator, and she was taken up to the sixth storey. When she lifted the brass knocker, Sebastian himself opened the door.

" I was expecting you," he said with a nod. " I knew you were in town, for I saw you in my audience last night, hiding behind a pillar. Did you like the concert? " He took her coat from her and hung it up. " Better take off your hat, too; you'll be more comfortable."

The music room opened directly off the entry hall, with only a doorway between. As she walked into it, Lucy noticed it was a big room, full of sunlight, and that the general colour was dark red; the rugs and curtains and chairs. The piano stood at the front, between two windows.

Sebastian saw that she was not looking at anything; probably she was frightened again.

"Shall we begin? We can talk afterwards. We'll work a little on the *Elijah*. I have to go to St. Paul to sing it with an oratorio society very soon, and I've not looked at it for a long while."

When she sat down at the piano, he put the music on the rack, turning over the pages. "Before we begin with my part, we might run through the tenor's aria, here. It's much too high for me, of course, but I like to sing it." He pointed to the page and began: "*If with all your heart you truly seek Him.*"

"That's a nice introduction to the whole thing, isn't it? Now we'll take it up just here," he leaned over her and indicated with his finger.

He walked up and down in his elkskin shoes as he sang, his hands in the pockets of his smoking-jacket. Lucy had no thought for anything but the score in front of her. An hour and a half went by very quickly. Just when she thought things were going better, he put his hand on her shoulder.

"Enough for today, Miss Gayheart. Very good for a first trial. Shall we begin at the same hour tomorrow? And don't become agitated when you make mistakes. What I most want is elasticity. You must learn to catch a hint quickly in the tempi. When I'm eccentric, catch step with me. I have a reason, or think I have. Now suppose we sit down over here by the fire and have a glass of port and a biscuit. We've been working very hard."

She rose and went to the chair he pointed out. She suddenly felt tired. Sebastian lowered the heavy window-shades a little, until the sunshine fell only on the rugs and the brass fire-irons. He brought a tray with a decanter and glasses and sat down opposite her, lounging back in his chair with his feet to the fire.

" Have you ever heard the *Elijah* well given, Miss Gayheart? "

Lucy told him she had never heard it given at all.

He smiled indulgently. " Mendelssohn is out of fashion just now. Who is the fashion? Debussy, I suppose? You've noticed that people are interested in music chiefly to have something to talk about at dinner parties? "

Lucy murmured she couldn't say as to that; she didn't go to dinner parties, and she didn't know anyone in Chicago except Professor Auerbach and a few of his students.

"And in your own part of the country isn't it so? "

" I think my father is the only person in our town who is much interested in music. He leads the town band and gives lessons on the clarinet."

" Your father is a music-teacher? "

" Not exactly. He's a watchmaker by trade, but he plays the clarinet and flute very well, and the violin a little."

" German, of course? That's good. A German watchmaker who plays the flute seems to me a comfortable sort of father to have."

He asked her how she happened to come to Chicago, and to study with Auerbach. She felt that his questions were not perfunctory, that he really wanted to know something about her life, and she got over her shyness.

While they were talking, the outer door opened softly, and a little man in a stiffly starched white jacket and noiseless tennis shoes, carrying several coats on hangers, darted through the room and disappeared into the sleeping-chamber beyond.

" That is Giuseppe, my valet," Sebastian explained. " Come in and see how well he does for me." He opened the door and took Lucy into his sleeping-room. " Giuseppe, this is the Signorina who is coming to play for me until Mr. Mockford is better. I want her to see how we live."

" *Si, si, signore.*" Giuseppe smiled eagerly and stepped back from the clothes-closet, pointing to the rows of coats and trousers very much as if he were a guide in a picture gallery. When he thought she had observed them sufficiently, he flourished

his hand toward the dressing-table and toward a
bed of faultless contour.

"Yes, he keeps everything very neat. If you
went through my bureau drawers, you'd find them
just like your own. He makes my breakfast too,
and brings it up to me."

Giuseppe stood holding his hands clasped in
front of his stomach, smiling like a little boy being praised. His face seemed almost like a boy's.
But his hair, Lucy noticed, was thin and faded, and
his high red forehead (shaped like a bowl) was
seamed by deep lines from left to right. A moment
later, when he had gone to the far end of the
music room to put fresh coal on the fire, Lucy
asked Sebastian whether Giuseppe had been with
him long.

"I picked him up in London, on the way over.
He used to be valet de chambre in an hotel in
Florence. I've never had better service. Think of
it, he has got all those lines on his forehead worry-
ing about other people's coats and boots and break-
fasts. I haven't a friend in the world who would
do for me what that little man would."

Something in the way he said this made Lucy
feel a trifle downcast. She almost wished she were
Giuseppe. After all, it was people like that who
counted with artists — more than their admirers.

When she left the studio a few moments later

she found the Italian in the little entrance hall, before a table drawer which was divided into compartments. Into these he was putting away gloves; into one white gloves, into another tan, into another grey. A man must be rich and successful indeed to live in such beautiful order, she thought.

When she reached her own room after lunch, she looked about it with affection and compassion. She pulled down the shades, opened the window a little, and threw herself upon the bed, too tired to sit up and too much excited to sleep. Things she had scarcely noticed at the time came rushing through her mind: the dressing-gown thrown on a chair, the silver on the dressing-table, the spongy softness of the rose-coloured blankets the valet was smoothing on the bed, and those gloves in the table drawer. Evidently nothing ever came near Sebastian to tarnish his personal elegance. She had never known a man who lived like that.

Harry Gordon was rich, to be sure; he owned carriages and blooded horses, sleighs and guns, and he had his clothes made in Chicago. But his things stood out, and weren't a part of himself. His overcoats were harsh to touch, his hats were stiff. He was crude, like everyone else she knew. An upstanding young man, they called him at home, easy and masterful in his own town, but in a big city he took on a certain self-importance, as if

he were afraid of being ignored in the crowd. She
remembered just how Sebastian looked when he
stood against the light in his heelless shoes and old
velvet jacket. He would be equal to any situation
in the world. He had a simplicity that must come
from having lived a great deal and mastered a
great deal. If you brushed against his life ever
so lightly it was like tapping on a deep bell; you
felt all that you could not hear.

7

It was settled that, for the present, Lucy should
go to the studio every day when Sebastian was in
town. In the morning she awoke with such lightness of heart that it seemed to her she had been
drifting on a golden cloud all night. After she had
lain still for a few moments to feel the physical
pleasure of coming up out of sleep, she would run
down a cold hallway and take her bath before the
other occupants on her floor were stirring. When
she entered the bakery downstairs, the savour of
coffee was delightful to her. Mrs. Schneff served
the early comers herself, in a blue gingham dress
and a white apron. She asked Lucy " how come "
she ate more breakfast now than she used to.
Lucy laughed and told her she was making more

money now. " Dat is goot," said the plump baker-
ess approvingly.

After breakfast Lucy went upstairs and put her
room in order. She could never make her bed
look so high and smooth as Giuseppe's, but that
was because she had no box-springs, or blankets
soft as fur.

The weather was miraculous, for January. She
always started very early for Michigan Avenue,
and had an hour or so to walk along the Lake
front before she went into the Arts Building.
There was very little ice in the water that January,
and the blue floor of the Lake, wrinkled with gold,
seemed to be the day itself, stretching before her
unspent and beautiful. As she walked along, holding her muff against her cheek on the wind side,
it was hard to believe there was anything in the
world she could not have if she wanted it. The
sharp air that blew off the water brought up all
the fire of life in her; it was like drinking fire. She
had to turn her back to it to catch her breath.

At ten o'clock she went into the studio and
brought the freshness of the morning weather to
a man who rose late and did not go abroad until
noon. She warmed her hands at the coal grate
while he finished his cigarette. If Sebastian had
been slow in dressing, Giuseppe answered her
knock, his dust-cloth on his arm, and hung up her

coat, telling her that the *maestro* would be out
subito, subito. He called her Signorina Lucia.
After she and Sebastian set to work, Giuseppe
went in to do the bedroom, leaving the door open
a little so that he could listen.

One morning when Sebastian finished singing
" *It is enough . . . I am not better than my
fathers,*" Lucy turned impulsively on her stool to
look at him. She never allowed herself to make
any comment (she knew he wouldn't like it), but
often she had to make some bodily movement to
break the tension. There in the doorway of the
sleeping-chamber stood Giuseppe, his red hands
crossed over his stomach, his head inclined, his
sharp face and quick little eyes melted into repose
and gravity. He caught up the laundry bag from
behind the door, and pausing just a moment on the
ball of his foot, looked Sebastian straight in the
eye. " *Ecco una cosa molto bella!* " he brought out
in a husky voice, before he vanished through the
entry hall.

Lucy found she clung to Giuseppe as if he were
a protector among things that were new and
strange. Several times she met him in the street,
going on errands in a grey overcoat much too long
for him and a hard felt hat. Or seeing her he would
snatch off his hat, and his face, his whole body,
indeed, would express astonishment and delight,

as if it were wonderful, almost supernatural, that
they should encounter one another thus.

Her acquaintance with Giuseppe progressed
rapidly, but with Sebastian she seemed to get little
further than on the first day. He kept well behind
his courteous, half-playful, and rather professional manner, — a manner so perfected that it
could go on representing him when he himself was
either lethargic or altogether absent. His ami-
ability puzzled Lucy, and rather discouraged her.

When she used to see Sebastian by chance occasionally, on the street or in the Park, his face
seemed to her forbidding. Sometimes she thought
it stern and indifferent, but more than once it had
struck her as melancholy. In the studio there was
none of that. He met her with a smile, and
throughout the morning was friendly and affable.
Yet she went away feeling that the other man,
whom she used to see secretly, was his real self.

Trivial, accidental things gradually broke down
his reserve. Once, as she was coming down the
Lake side of Michigan Avenue, just before she
crossed to the Arts Building, she happened to
glance up, and saw Sebastian standing at an open
window, looking down at her. He leaned out a little and waved his hand. After that he was at the
window almost every morning. This made a difference in the way he greeted her at the door; it

was as if they had already met in the street and
were coming into the studio together. There was
a keener interest in his eyes when he took her hand,
and he looked down into her face as if she were
bringing him something that pleased him. He once
told her so, indeed. She had just put her hat
on the hall table. He took it up, stroked the brown
fur, and ran his finger-tips along the slender,
drooping red feather.

"You know, I like to see this little red feather
coming down the street. I watch for it, and should
be terribly disappointed if it didn't come. You
seem to find walking in the cold the most delightful thing imaginable. Montaigne says somewhere
that in early youth the joy of life lies in the feet.
You recall that passage to me, Lucy. I had forgotten it."

He often told her amusing stories. It was not a
habit of his, but he liked to hear her laugh. He
never remarked upon this (compliments, he believed, had a disastrous effect upon any charming
natural expression), but he provoked it for his
own pleasure. A beautiful laugh was rare, certainly; after she left him he used to screw up his
eyes and try to imitate it in his mind. Nothing
about her drew him to her so much as this purely
unconscious physical response.

Lucy knew more or less about Sebastian's outside life from his telephone conversations. When she left the piano, he always made her rest before she went out into the cold. He sat down and talked to her, but they were very often interrupted by the telephone, — the house operator put no calls through until after eleven-thirty. Lucy could not help hearing his replies and learning something about his engagements, his business affairs, who his friends were. With women his talk was usually gentle and soothing, as if the lady at the other end were in a flurry, or very insistent. He told the most transparent lies in refusing invitations, didn't seem to try to make them plausible. But he always said something agreeable; asked to be remembered to the lady's charming daughter, or thanked her for recommending a book which he had liked very much. Every day his concert agent, Morris Weisbourn, called him up as soon as his wire was open. Their talk was usually very brief. But one morning when he answered Weisbourn's call Lucy heard a sudden change in Sebastian's voice.

"What's that, Morris? When did this letter come? . . . No, she wrote me nothing about it. We don't discuss business matters in our correspondence, that is what you are for. . . . Send a draft for the amount she mentions, and get it off today, not later. . . . Of course I can. Simply let the bills go over. . . . Very well, then meet me at the Auditorium for lunch, and I'll write a cheque for it."

When he came back from the telephone he lit another cigarette and took up the story he had been telling her about his first meeting with Debussy. But there was something bleak and unnatural in his smile, and Lucy hurried away.

She knew, as well as if a name had been mentioned, that the woman who had written for money was Mrs. Sebastian, and she thought it a shame. He always spoke of his wife in a very chivalrous way, and admiringly. She had heard him explain over the telephone, to a friend just arrived from the Orient, that Mrs. Sebastian was not with him because she dreaded the Chicago winter climate. When he happened to tell Lucy about something he and his wife had done or seen, he seemed to recall it with pleasure, became animated and gay. But she felt sure that things were not like that with them now. Perhaps this was why he was unhappy.

His manner, when she was with him, was that of a man who has an easy, if somewhat tolerant, enjoyment of life. Some of the people who telephoned him he seemed really fond of, and she knew that he was attached to James Mockford, " one of the few friends who have lasted through time and change," as he once remarked. But he seemed very careful never to come too close to people. She believed he was disappointed in something — or in everything.

She had been playing for him nearly three weeks, when quite by accident she saw again that side of him which his genial manner usually covered. One evening Giuseppe knocked at her door, bringing a note from Sebastian. He would not be at the studio tomorrow morning, as he had to attend the funeral services of a friend.

Lucy looked through the evening paper and found that Madame Renée de Vignon, a French singer, returning from California, had died in her hotel last night after an illness of only twenty-four hours. There would be a funeral service for her at eleven o'clock in the small Catholic church near her hotel. Afterwards her body would be sent back to France.

The next morning, a little before the hour announced, Lucy stole into the church. There were not a great many people there, and in the dusky light she easily found Sebastian. He was kneeling, with his hand over his face. When the organ began to play softly, and the doors were opened and held back to admit the pallbearers, he lifted his head and turned in his seat to face the coffin, carried into the church on the shoulders of six men. A company of priests and censer-bearers went with

it up the aisle toward the altar. As it moved forward, Sebastian's eyes never left it; turning his
head slowly, he followed it with a look that struck
a chill to Lucy's heart. It was a terrible look;
anguish and despair, and something like entreaty.
All faces were turned reverently toward the procession, but his stood out from the rest with a feeling personal and passionate. He had forgotten
himself, forgotten where he was and that there
were people who might stare at him. It seemed to
Lucy that a wave of black despair had swept into
the church, carrying him and that black coffin up
the aisle together, while the clergy and worship-
pers were unconscious of it. Had this woman been
a very dear friend? Or was it death itself that
seemed horrible to him — death in a foreign land,
in a hotel, far from everything one loved?

During the service he remained kneeling. From
time to time he drew out a handkerchief and wiped
his forehead, but he did not lift his face or his
broad black shoulders until the coffin was carried
back toward the door. As it passed him, he gave it
one long, dull look, out of half-closed eyes. He was
among the first to leave the church. When Lucy
reached the steps outside, she could see him far
down the street, walking rapidly, his back straight
and stiff.

Once before, in November (how long ago it

seemed!), she had seen him coming out of a church, the Cathedral, when she happened to be passing. He merely came out of the door, down the steps, and turned straight north, without looking about for a cab as he usually did. She felt sure, by the look on his face, that he was coming from some religious observance. She went into the Cathedral; there was no service going on, there were not a dozen people in the building; but she knew that he had been there with a purpose that had to do with the needs of his soul.

8

Usually Sebastian and Mockford went out of town at the end of the week to give a recital somewhere. Sebastian often telephoned the young man, making appointments for the evening or afternoon, but Mockford never dropped in upon them in the morning, and Lucy was glad of it. She had never met him, or seen him except on the concert stage. One morning when Sebastian handed her some songs from *Die Winterreise* and asked her to look them over, she sighed and shook her head.

" It won't be much use, I'm afraid. After hearing Mr. Mockford play them, I think the best I can do is just to read them off."

Sebastian laughed. "Jimmy is a little genius with those, isn't he? I doubt if Schubert ever heard them played so well. In his mind, perhaps. Jimmy's not especially good with Mozart or the Italian composers; but in the true German Lieder, whatever he does seems to be right. I've got a great many hints from him."

On the day Sebastian was to leave for his concert engagements in Minnesota and Wisconsin, Lucy went to the studio to tell him good-bye. It was Mockford who opened the door for her and asked her to come in. She drew back and would have run away if she could.

"No, come in, Miss Gayheart. It is Miss Gayheart, isn't it? Clément has gone down to Allston's studio for a moment. Please allow me." He took her coat, waited for her to go into the music room, and limped in after her.

While he was pulling up a chair for her and poking the coal fire, she saw him by daylight for the first time. She had thought of him as a very young man, a youth, indeed. This morning he did not seem young, but wiry and rather hard. Even his white skin looked harder, somewhat rubbery, and there was a yellow glint in it where the razor had not bit close. His copper-red hair fitted his head so snugly that it might have been a well-made wig.

" I'm glad to meet you, Miss Gayheart. Glad to have an opportunity to thank you for filling in." He sat down and looked at Lucy, looked her over deliberately, and she looked at him. When they had met at the door, the light was behind him and she could not see his eyes. They might be called hazel, perhaps, but this morning they were frankly green; a cool, sparkling green, with something restless in them. He was the first to break down in the searching look they gave each other. He rose quickly and softly and lowered the window-shades a little. On the way back to his chair, he began talking:

" I'm very upset to be fussing with doctors and dropping out like this. Neither of us had looked forward to this American season with much pleasure. However, he seems to be getting on very well with you."

" I don't know as to that. I've no experience. I do the best I can." Lucy could not tell whether he meant to be patronizing, or whether he was merely ill at ease. She felt that he had disliked her instantly, as she had him.

" Oh, he rather fancies breaking in a new person. The difficulty is that Clément can never work with anyone who isn't personally sympathetic to him. The odds are always against our being able to pick up one of that sort on short notice."

Lucy flushed, but said nothing. She was looking at his white, freckled hands, lying on the red velvet arms of the chair. The fingers were square and unusually short for a pianist, but the breadth of palm was remarkable.

" He gives a good account of you " — Mockford shot her a green glance — " and since you do get on, it may be a good thing for him — a change. He doesn't find much to divert him here. The truth is, he's bored to death. I wasn't for his coming over at all. But he needs the money. And he'd be bored anywhere just now. It's only fair to say that you're not hearing the artist we know at home and on the Continent."

" You have been with him a long while, Mr. Mockford? "

" Yes, off and on, a long while," he said carelessly. " There have been interregnums. Mrs. Sebastian takes a fancy to a new pianist now and then, and Clément tries him out. So far they've not been altogether satisfactory."

" She is musical then, Mrs. Sebastian? "

" Oh, naturally! She is one of Sir Robert Lester's daughters." He glanced at Lucy to see whether this enlightened her. It did not, so he murmured: " He was one of our best conductors. The pianist has to make it go with her as well as with Clément, if you mean that."

Lucy coloured again. " No, I did not mean that.
I only wanted to know if she is much interested in
— in that side of him."

" In all sides, I should say. She was accustomed
to direct things in her father's household. It be-
comes her very well." He wrinkled up his short
nose and squinted as if a strong light had been
flashed in his face.

There was a kind of fascination about Mockford, Lucy thought. He looked as if he were made
up for the stage, yet there he sat in perfectly conventional clothes, except for a green silk shirt and
green necktie. He couldn't help looking theatrical; he was made so, and she couldn't tell whether
or not he liked being unusual. His manner was a
baffling mixture of timidity and cheek. One thing
was clear; he was uncomfortable in her company,
and certainly she was in his. She was about to rise
when she heard a fumbling at the door. It was not
Sebastian, however, but the hall porter, with the
railway tickets. He gave them to Mockford, told
him at what hour their train left, and just when he
would have a cab downstairs for them.

As soon as he was gone, Lucy rose and said she
couldn't wait. She wished them both a pleasant
journey, and would Mr. Sebastian please let her
know if he needed her again?

" He will telegraph you, doubtless. We shall be

gone eight days or more; two oratorios and three recitals. He'll be disappointed at missing you, but he's very apt to forget engagements."

Lucy went down in the elevator, wondering whether she would ever go up in it again.

She had dreaded meeting Mockford, but she couldn't have imagined that such a meeting would break her courage and hurt her feelings. She fiercely resented his having any opinions about her or her connection with Sebastian. This was the first time a third person had in any way come upon their little scene, and she hated it. So they had talked her over. Natural perhaps, but it hurt her, all the same. There was something else that disturbed her. She felt that this strange man who was neither young nor old, who was picturesque and a little repelling, was not altogether trustworthy. If she had encouraged him, he would have talked to her too freely about Mrs. Sebastian, and he spoke of Sebastian in a tone that was objectionably familiar. He struck her as terribly selfish and vain, and jealous of the man he called " Clément." She wished she could get his white face out of her mind.

As she hurried along the street, she thought of one mistake after another. Mockford had made her see her position as an outsider must see it. He had made her feel that an inexperienced country girl, with no education, shouldn't be trying to do his work for him.

Why, then, hadn't they got a professional accompanist? There were plenty of them in Chicago. It was a farce, that she should be playing for Sebastian; just how had she ever got in for it? She had gone to his studio the first time because she was asked to come; she loved being there, and went again and again. He had seemed pleased and amused, and was very kind. She even felt that he liked her being young and ignorant and not too clever. It was an accidental relationship, between someone who had everything and someone who had nothing at all; and it concerned nobody else. She had dropped down into the middle of this man's life, and she snatched what she could, from the present and the past. Her playing for him was nothing but make-believe; and his friendliness was make-believe, perhaps. Then there was nothing real about it, — except her own feeling. That was real.

That afternoon Lucy had to give two lessons at Auerbach's studio. While she was there the weather changed and a sullen winter rain set in. She was used to walking home in the rain; she left the studio and set off in the right direction. But after a while she found herself facing east instead of west, and very soon she was on the far side of Michigan Avenue. She walked up and down opposite the Arts Building, watching the lights in Sebastian's windows. After a time the windows went dark. She saw the hall porter carry out a steamer trunk on his shoulder and strap it on the back of a cab. Sebastian and Mockford followed him and stood talking under the awning while the bags were brought down. Then Sebastian tipped the porter and the bag boy, shepherded the lame man into the cab, got in after him, and drove away. Lucy felt discouraged and alone in the world.

She went slowly across the town, getting a kind of comfort out of the crowded streets and the people who rushed by and bumped into her, hurrying away from the rain. In the city you had plenty of room to be lonely, no one noticed, she reflected. And if you were burning yourself up, so was everyone else; you weren't smouldering alone on the edge of the prairie. She thought she had never before seen so many sad and discouraged people. Tramps, wet as the horses, stood in the empty doorways for shelter. She passed an old man steaming himself in the vapour that rose from an iron grating in the sidewalk.

Usually Lucy went through these streets with her mind racing ahead of her, like a little boy following a balloon, not minding the cold for herself or for anyone else. But tonight all these people seemed like companions, and she felt a kind of humble affection for them.

9

Sebastian had been away nine days, and Lucy began to wonder whether he would ever need her again. He had sent her a cheque, without any word, in a note written to Auerbach. It was much too large, and made her feel as if she were being paid off. She hadn't cashed it; it lay in her top bureau drawer.

She had been very busy; had managed to get in four lessons with Auerbach, besides giving the usual time to her pupils, and she had practised resolutely. But her heart was not in it. Probably he had found a pianist who suited him better, or perhaps James Mockford felt well enough to take up his work again. That day at the studio, when Mockford was standing behind her holding her coat, she had happened to glance at the mirror over the table and caught a strange smile flickering over his face; as if he had a safe card up his sleeve.

On the tenth morning of Sebastian's absence Lucy awoke late because the room was dark. It was storming outside, and there was a snowdrift on her floor beneath the open window. She put on her dressing-gown, swept up the snow with a whisk-broom and a newspaper, turned on the heat, and got back into bed to wait until the room was warm. As she lay there thinking of nothing in particular, she was startled by a knock on her door, and a boy's voice called: " Western Union! "

When the rubber-caped boy was gone, Lucy stood looking at the yellow envelope before she tore it open. She felt sure that it was from Sebastian, and it happened to be the first telegram she had ever received in her life.

Hope you can be at the studio Thursday morning usual hour. Greetings.

Sebastian

Thursday; that was tomorrow. Lucy stuck the telegram in her mirror and hurriedly began to dress. She was thinking that years from now, when she would probably be teaching piano to the neighbours' children in Haverford, nothing would recall this part of her life so vividly, or make it seem so real, as that slip of paper.

When she went down to the bakery Mrs. Schneff greeted her with a broad smile. " You eat a good breakfast today, I expect? The telegraph boy come in here to inquire, but I see you ain't got no bad news anyway."

No, Lucy told her, it was something pleasant.

"Dat's good. Now you eat a good breakfast. I don't like to see you git worried like." She wiped off a table with her apron, and spread a clean napkin over it.

A little later Lucy put on her high overshoes and hurried to the bank to cash her cheque. Then she went to a department store and bought a new dress for the studio, a pretty one, with a silk blouse and embroidered jacket. As she walked home, carrying her parcels with her, she stopped at a flower shop and got a bunch of violets.

She spent the afternoon putting her clothes and bureau drawers in order. At four o'clock she went over to Auerbach's studio to give a lesson. When she came back, her room was almost dark; the air was fresh from the window she had left a little open, and full of the smell of violets. Like spring, it was, to one coming in out of the wintry streets. She sat down in the dusk before the grey square of window-glass to rest.

Yesterday she had been like someone waiting in a doctor's office; it was not living, it was time passing. There was a strange heaviness under whatever she did, as if she had swallowed lead. Today everything was soft, tranquil. There was a kindness in the air one breathed. Everyone in the shops had seemed kind. Life ought always to be like this.

Presently, when even the square of window was dark, she lit the gas and sat down at the piano, beginning to play over some songs from *Die schöne Müllerin,* which Sebastian had been practising before he left. She was thinking that he must be already on his way home, settled in his stateroom and rushing through the great snowy country up there . . . full of forests and lakes, she had heard tell.

10

The city was very sloppy on the morning after the snow-storm, and Lucy did not take her usual walk along the Lake; she was afraid of splashing her new dress. She went straight to the Arts Building. How glad she was to greet the hall porter, and to step into the elevator once more!

" I haven't bothered you for some time, have I, George? Mr. Sebastian is home again? "

"Yes, miss. He got in early yesterday morning."

Lucy was astonished. He got back yesterday? Why, the telegram had come yesterday, saying he would arrive today — but no, the message didn't really say that, she remembered. He must have sent it just before he got on the train at St. Paul. She hadn't noticed the date. How strange, when he could have sent her word from this building yesterday! However, that was probably his way of doing things, — and she was already at the studio door.

Sebastian opened it, in his elkskins and short jacket as usual, but he looked younger and fresher than when he went away. He laughed as she came in, and dropped both hands lightly on her shoulders.

"And here she is! Let me have a look at you, and tell me whether you have been a good girl all this while. A new dress, too; such a pretty one! "

While he detained her in the entry hall, she vaguely noticed a heavy fragrance of fresh flowers in the air. Going into the music room, she saw that the tea table had been moved from its usual place beside the coal grate, and on it stood a large primrose-tinted vase, full of cream-coloured roses and heavy, drooping sprays of acacia. She exclaimed and stopped to look at them on her way to the piano. They were rich and opulent beyond anything she had ever seen.

"Yes, a kind lady, an old friend, stopped over in Chicago yesterday and called on me. This morning, on her way to the train, she brought me those, just as they are."

Lucy had never seen mimosa except in florists' windows, and she lingered over it; it seemed like a whole garden from the South. " I think that lady must have been a sweetheart," she murmured.

Sebastian smiled. " Perhaps. And perhaps she remembers things as sweeter than they were. That often happens. And it's a mercy, too ! " He was arranging the music for her. "We will begin *Die schöne Müllerin* and go straight along until we are tired. I feel like work this morning."

She thought she had never heard him sing so beautifully, but she was much too timid to say so. He went through the cycle before he stopped. Then he brought out his bottle of port and they sat down before the fire. He began to tell her about his concerts in the North, and said he liked engagements with singing societies.

" Many singers don't, you know. But I always feel such a friendliness in the people of the chorus; and I like them, especially when they sing well. In Minneapolis the sopranos were very good. The basses, too; most of them Germans and Swedes. The people in choral societies really get something out of music, something to help them through their lives, not something to talk about. Plumbers and brewers and bank clerks and dressmakers, they wouldn't be there unless it meant something; it cuts one night out of their week all winter."

Just then he was called to the telephone to speak

with his agent. When he came back, Lucy was again bending over the flowers. He picked up the vase and stood holding it between himself and the light.

"Yes, they're nice, aren't they? Very suggestive: youth, love, hope — all the things that pass." He turned around to the fire and took up the cigarette he had left on the mantel.

In that moment while he seemed absent-minded Lucy slipped into the hall and put on her coat and hat. She came back to say good-bye. He was still standing by the grate, smoking, more approachable than usual; but when he took her hand he was clearly thinking about something else.

"Mr. Sebastian," she asked him, her face breaking into a smile, "didn't you ever get any pleasure out of being in love?"

He shook his head slowly, frowned with his brows and smiled with his lips. "N-n-no, not much." Then turning to find an ash-tray, he said mischievously: "Why? — Do you?"

Lucy found herself at the door with her hand on the knob. She wanted nothing so much as to be outside, but for some reason she stopped and turned to face him, without seeing him at all.

"Yes, I do. And nobody can spoil it."

She could hear her own voice, small and cracked because there was no breath behind it. Once out-

side the door she did not ring for the elevator, but
ran down the five flights of stairs as fast as she
could.

When she was a little girl she used to run away
after she had been scolded, along the country road
that led toward the Platte, faster and faster, as if
she could leave hurt feelings behind. Now in the
same way she went hurrying across the city, splashing the new dress she had meant to take care of.
She was crying, and she did not care who saw her.
She would never go back to the studio. If she
couldn't keep her feelings to herself, she must stay
away. All the same, it was heartless of him to
make fun of her; it was just the kind of thing she
would never have expected of him. He had been
seeing a woman who was rich and beautiful and
cultivated, who had everything that she had not.
His spirits were high, and his vanity had been flattered; he found Lucy Gayheart amusing. The moment she saw those flowers she had felt a sudden
uneasiness, and a vague envy of the unknown person who had a right to send him roses worth their
weight in gold. Until today she could not have imagined that he would ever be unkind to her; indifferent, perhaps, but not unkind. Moreover, he was
mistaken. She didn't care for him in that way.
She didn't want anything from him; she didn't
even want him to be too much aware of her. Why
had he said that?

Book I

When Lucy was almost home she suddenly stopped and stood still, looked down into the mud with intense amazement on her face. It was quite possible that he had not meant at all what she thought! What did he know about her life, after all? He might easily take it for granted that she had a sweetheart among the students. She was pretty, at an age when it is quite natural to be in love. Older men often teased young girls in that way as a compliment. Her shoulders relaxed, and she walked on slowly.

Then perhaps everything was all right, or would be but for that stupid speech she had made at the door. Oh, why had she exposed her wound and her anger! How often Pauline had told her that one day she would come to grief from blurting out everything she felt.

She had not been in her own room half an hour when a messenger boy came with a telegram. He said the answer was prepaid, and he must wait for it. She tore open the envelope with a feeling of dread. It was from Sebastian, asking whether she could meet him for tea at the Auditorium at five o'clock. He added the word " important."

She couldn't, just then, bear the thought of seeing him. Fortunately, she had a sound reason for refusing. She wrote a truthful answer.

" I am sorry, but I have to give a lesson for Professor Auerbach at five."

She did not want to sign her name, but the messenger boy insisted that it was necessary. After he was gone, she looked from the yellow sheet in her hand to the other telegram on her dresser, which had come only yesterday. What had happened in the meantime? She gave it up; she was too tired to think. Let chance take its way. She lay down and slept for nearly two hours. When she got up at four o'clock to go to Auerbach's studio she was quite herself again.

Lucy kept her pupil longer than usual that afternoon. Mr. Auerbach came to the door and asked her to stop at his study before she left the building. When she went there, she found Clement Sebastian seated by Auerbach's desk, talking to him. He rose as she entered and held out his hand. He said he wanted to see her about tomorrow's work, and as she had no telephone he had thought he might reach her through Auerbach. " I have a cab waiting outside, so I may as well take you home, we can talk on the way. And now I shall find where this young lady lives, Paul. To me her number indicates the middle of the Chicago River."

When they were seated in the cab he came to the point at once.

" Now, my dear, whatever did you mean by flying off like that this morning? One is always saying things of that sort to young people. It's not in very good taste, perhaps, but it's customary, and we've grown used to it — surely *you* must be used to it! Why were you so annoyed?"

Lucy looked out of the carriage window. She found it rather difficult to explain.

"I don't know, Mr. Sebastian. I felt ashamed afterwards. I think it must have been something in the way you said it. I was startled. Please never think of it again. I know you didn't mean anything unkind."

"Unkind? Lucy, my dear! Come, we must trust each other more than that. We mustn't have little clouds creeping over our mornings. We can't afford it. Sailing dates come soon enough, and then we'll be sorry."

As they turned a corner the green lights of the bakery windows came into view. In a moment the cab stopped.

"So this is where you live! If you won't come over to me for tea, I shall come here and have coffee with you. A very substantial place it looks." He accompanied her to the foot of the linoleum-covered wooden stairs and stood for a moment, holding his hat in his hand and smiling down into her face. His eyes still had that livelier look she had noticed in the morning. "Till tomorrow, then? And I'll be as solemn as an owl. No joking with Lucy!"

The next morning it was Giuseppe who opened
the door for her, beaming and rapidly exploding
into speech. By this time she could understand him
pretty well. Sebastian had given her an Italian
grammar one day, and told her she might as well
pick up what she could. Giuseppe explained that
Sebastian had been called upstairs to see Signor
Cunningham, who was ill, but would return in a
moment. Meanwhile she must sit down and get
warm. He dropped on his knees and began blowing the fire. Then he went on with his dusting, telling her all the while what good fortune it was for
her, so young, to work with a great artist like
Sebastian. Education was everything in this world;
if his father had been able to send him to school,
he would not now *fare il cameriere*. For the first
time it occurred to Lucy that even this smiling
little man might have his regrets. And had he, in
his uncanny way, sensed that something went
wrong yesterday?

II

One Sunday afternoon near the end of February Lucy was sitting in her room looking out at
the back of the next building, which came close to
her window, — a blank wall of bricks painted

grey. Sunday was the only day in which she had much time for reflection. She gave lessons all day on Saturday, but on Sunday she was free.

This morning she was wondering how a month, nearly two months, indeed, could have slipped by so quickly. A strange kind of life she had been leading. For two hours, five days of the week, she was alone with Sebastian, shut away from the rest of the world. It was as if they were on the lonely spur of a mountain, enveloped by mist. They saw no one but Giuseppe, heard no one; the city below was blotted out. Then, after eleven-thirty, the city began poking in its fingers. The telephone began to buzz, and she heard him build up the rest of his day and his evening. At about twelve she got into the elevator and dropped down into Chicago again.

The weather, which everyone grumbled about, had been exactly the right weather for her. The dark, stormy mornings made the warmth and quiet toward which she hurried seem all the richer. The dirty streets, as she crossed the town through sleet and snow, were like narrow rivers, shut in by grey cliffs where the light was always changing, and she herself was a twig or a leaf swept along on the current. As soon as she reached the studio, that excitement and sense of struggle vanished; her mind was like a pair of dancing balances brought to rest. Something quieted her like a great natural force. Things took on their right relation, the trivial and disturbing shut out. Life was resolved into something simple and noble — yes, and joyous; a joyousness which seemed safe from time or change, like that in Schubert's *Die Forelle*, which Sebastian often sang.

Lucy stopped looking at the streaks of rain against the grey wall, went to her shabby piano, and played that song again and again. There were other songs which she associated more closely with Sebastian himself, but this one was like the studio, like the hours they spent there together. No matter where in the world she should ever hear it, it would always drop her down again into that room with the piano between two big windows, the coal fire glowing behind her, the Lake reaching out before her, and the man walking carelessly up and down as he sang.

On this same Sunday Sebastian himself was going through a bad time. He happened to have no out-of-town engagement, so he was in Chicago, in his studio. This day, with a brutal rain beating on brutal buildings, had been one of slowly rising misery.

In the morning paper he had read a dispatch from Geneva, announcing the death of an old friend and fellow student, at a sanatorium in

Savoy. He hadn't even known that Larry Mac-
Gowan was ill; there had been a coldness between
them for the last few years. But the moment his
eyes fell on that black headline the feeling of
estrangement vanished as if it had never been. The
reality was their ardent, generous young friendship, their student days together — which were
only yesterday, after all. He put down the newspaper softly, as if he were afraid of wakening
someone. It was like reading his own death notice.
Like it? It was just that. The obituary would serve
for both — for their good days.

Nothing had ever made Sebastian admit to himself that his youth was forever and irrevocably
gone. He had clung to a secret belief that he would
pick it up again, somewhere. This was a time of
temporary lassitude and disillusion, but his old
feeling about life would come back; he would turn
a corner and confront it. He would waken some
morning and step out of bed the man he used to be.
Now, all in a moment, it came over him that when
people spoke of their dead youth they were not
using a figure of speech. The thing he was looking
for had gone out into the wide air, like a volatile
essence, and he was staring into the empty jar.
Emptiness, that was the feeling: the very objects
in his studio seemed to draw farther apart, and to
regard each other more coldly. MacGowan had

slipped out of all this; grey skies, falling rain, chilled affections. Everything in this room, in this city and this country, had suddenly become unfamiliar and unfriendly.

The lid once off, he began remembering everything, and everything seemed to have gone wrong. Life had so turned out that now, when he was nearing fifty, he was without a country, without a home, without a family, and very nearly without friends. Surely a man couldn't congratulate himself upon a career which had led to such results. He had missed the deepest of all companionships, a relation with the earth itself, with a countryside and a people. That relationship, he knew, cannot be gone after and found; it must be long and deliberate, unconscious. It must, indeed, be a way of living. Well, he had missed it, whatever it was, and he had begun to believe it the most satisfying tie men can have. Friendships? Larry was the man he had cared for most. Among women? There was little for sweet reflection in that chapter. He had married the woman he loved, and for years they had been happy; now they were both better off when they had the Atlantic between them. The thing which had estranged them was not at all the conventional situation supposed to arise between an artist and his wife. It was jealousy, perhaps, but not of the usual sort.

As they had no children, Sebastian had taken

into their house a talented boy, almost a child when he came, who had no home and no parents; the orphan of a couple who had both sung at the Opéra Comique. He was a charming boy, and devoted to Madame Sebastian. But she had taken a strong dislike to him and treated him harshly. The lad was sensitive, and so adoring of her that her severity amounted to cruelty. After a year and a half Sebastian could endure the situation no longer, and sent Marius away to a good school. But this did not mend matters; he had seen a side of his wife's nature which he had never before suspected; it had changed his feeling for her. She sensed this, and was bitter. He missed the boy and used to go into Paris to see him; even this she resented. He came to America, to Chicago, where he was born, though he had left it at eighteen and had lived abroad most of the time since.

Sebastian had been sitting by the fire for hours. He had smoked until his throat was dry, and his thoughts had wandered over a great part of the surface of the earth. He had dragged the bottom, and brought up nothing worth remembering. His mind could not find a comfortable position to lie in. He remembered Macbeth's, *Oh, full of scorpions is my mind, dear wife!* Wasn't there one lovely, unspoiled memory? — In the present wasn't there somewhere a flower or a green bough

that he could hold close and breathe its freshness?
His glance wandered toward the piano; perhaps
there was one!

Sebastian got up and opened the windows wide,
wound a scarf about his throat, and walked up and
down the room while the wind blew out the tobacco smoke. He was thinking about Lucy; that
perhaps he wouldn't have got so far down this
morning if she had been there for an hour. It was
dangerous to go for sympathy to a young girl who
was in love with one, but Lucy was different. As he
paced back and forth he told himself that hers was
quite another kind of feeling than the one he had
encountered under so many disguises. It seemed
complete in itself, not putting out tentacles all the
while. He had sometimes thought of her as rather
boyish, because she was so square. It was more like
a chivalrous loyalty than a young passion. He
didn't believe she would ever be guilty of those
uncatalogued, faint treacheries which vanity
makes young people commit. He didn't believe she
would ever use his name for her own advantage —
not even in a harmless way, to make herself interesting to a crowd of students, for instance. That
was a good deal to say for a young thing with her
living to make, struggling to get a foothold in a
slippery world. He hadn't met with just that kind
of delicacy before, in man or woman. When she

gave him a quick shy look and the gold sparks
flashed in her eyes, he read devotion there, and the
fire of imagination; but no invitation, no appeal.
In her companionship there was never the shadow
of a claim. On the contrary, there was a spirit
whicn disdained advantage.

He suddenly noticed that the place had grown
very cold. His watch said five o'clock; he must
have been on his feet for nearly an hour. The air
of the room had freshened, and something within
him had freshened. The contraction in his chest,
the bitter taste in his mouth were gone. He shut
the windows and went into his bedroom to change
his clothes. In a quarter of an hour he came out in
a dinner jacket and put on his overcoat. Downstairs he hailed the first cab he saw and gave the
driver Lucy's number.

When he got out before the bakery he told the
cabman to wait. First he glanced into the restaurant, thinking she might already have come down
for her supper. Then he went up the two flights of
stairs. He would not have known at which door to
knock, but behind one of them he heard a piano
with a bad tone; *Die Forelle*. He smiled, and when
she had finished he knocked gently.

"Who is it?"

"It's Sebastian, Miss Gayheart. May I see you
for a moment?"

Lucy glanced despairingly about the room; but it was dark, he couldn't see anything. She pulled her dressing-gown tight and opened the door a little way.

"I shouldn't bother you on Sunday, should I? But won't you come out to dinner with me tonight, if you've no other engagement? I've had a melancholy day, and I dread dining alone."

"Why, certainly, Mr. Sebastian. I'll have to dress, but it won't take long."

"Don't hurry, take all the time you want. It's still very early. I'll wait for you downstairs in the cab. And I'll go into the bakery and buy a bun, so the good woman can see that you are driving off with a staid, respectable person."

Lucy shut the door and lit the gas. She had only the same old evening dress, the black net she had worn to all his concerts. However, she told herself, if it was well-dressed women he wished to dine with, there were plenty he could ask. He must know she hadn't any clothes, and if he didn't mind, she didn't. —But she would have given a great deal to have a new dress to put on for him.

When they went into the hotel dining-room she was glad to find that it was nearly empty; he wouldn't have to conduct a shabby girl through a roomful of smart people. While they were waiting for the soup he smiled for the first time.

"I'm afraid I startled you, turning up uninvited

like that. I've been sticking in the studio all day. Did you happen to notice in the morning paper that Larry MacGowan died yesterday in a sanatorium in Savoy? We were the closest of friends, long ago. We were students together."

The day of Madame de Vignon's funeral flashed up in Lucy's mind. She could only murmur that she was sorry he had had bad news.

"And I am sorry in the wrong way. I am sorry for myself. Years ago if I had seen that thing in brutal type, I would have lain down and cried like a boy. Things happen to our friendships; that's the worst about living. Young people can't know what it means."

The waiter came with the soup and wine. When he was gone, Sebastian began to talk again.

"We had drifted apart, and for no good reason. Five years ago he came to visit me in France. My wife and I had been having our little place at Chantilly done over, and we were very pleased with it. I had looked forward to Larry's visit, but it didn't turn out well. He didn't like our house or our servants or our friends, or anything else. He showed it plainly, and I was disappointed and piqued. Our parting was cold. I think he must have been breaking up even then. He was difficult about everything, and he made criticisms that hurt one's feelings."

"Did you never see him afterwards?"

"Never. Other troubles came along, soon enough. We exchanged a few letters, the kind which mean nothing. The dispatch said he died in a sanatorium in the mountains above Sallanches. He and I took a walking trip through that very country one summer when we were in our early twenties. He must have recalled those days, when he was ill up there. We used to lie down on the hillsides and look up at those mountains, with our knapsacks under our heads, for hours together. We always got up very early and went out on our balconies before sunrise, while the light was changing on the peaks, and called good-morning to each other. I can't help wondering why he didn't wish to see me again. Why didn't he send for me last summer, I wonder?"

Sebastian drank a good deal of wine, and he told Lucy more about his own life than he had ever done before: how he had met Larry MacGowan on the steamer when he first left Chicago and was on his way abroad to study. He soon found that MacGowan also was going over to study, and under the same master. When they landed at Cherbourg they were already friends. They took a studio together in Paris and lived at the same pension.

Sebastian lingered a long while over his dinner. The dining-room was almost empty when they at last left it and took a cab for Lucy's part of the town. He slipped his arm through hers and pressed her hand gratefully. "You were kind to give me this evening, Lucy. I wanted to talk to someone; and I wanted it to be you. No one else."

She turned to him quickly and caught his sleeve. "Oh, Mr. Sebastian, I wish you didn't ever have to be sad! I am happy whenever I think about you, and so are lots of people. You have everything other people are struggling for. You don't value it enough, truly you don't!" She stopped because she knew she was talking foolishly.

Sebastian was listening not to what she said, but to the rush of feeling in her warm young voice. There is no way to define that ring of truth in a voice, he was thinking, and no mistaking it. He took the hand on his sleeve and held it between both his own. "Do I seem sad to you, Lucy? Everyone has disappointments. I'm sometimes lonely over here. Not in the mornings, when we are working together; then I feel quite like myself. That reminds me: tomorrow morning I must spend with my agent. Perhaps you can come in at five o'clock and have tea with me? I should like that."

The cab turned the corner, and the greenish-white lights in the bakery windows came into view. Sebastian took her to the foot of the stairway

" Remember," he said, " tomorrow is a holiday
for you, and you are to sleep late and dream of
something very nice. Perhaps you will dream that
we are both twenty, and are taking a walking trip
in the French Alps. And I shall call to you at daybreak from my balcony ! "

1 2

The next afternoon Lucy was walking slowly
over toward Michigan Avenue. She had never
loved the city so much; the city which gave one the
freedom to spend one's youth as one pleased, to
have one's secret, to choose one's master and serve
him in one's own way. Yesterday's rain had left
a bitter, springlike smell in the air; the vehemence that beat against her in the street and
hummed above her had something a little wistful in it tonight, like a plaintive hand-organ tune.
All the lovely things in the shop windows, the
furs and jewels, roses and orchids, seemed to
belong to her as she passed them. Not to have
wrapped up and sent home, certainly; where
would she put them? But they were hers to live
among.

At last it was five o'clock, the grey twilight
was gone, and she turned toward the Arts Build-

ing. She was frightened as she went up in the elevator, and tried not to think at all. She lifted the brass knocker, and Sebastian opened the door. Before she had time to speak, just as she was, in her hat and coat, he took her in his arms.

They stood for a long while without moving, in the dusky little hall among overcoats and walking-sticks. Lucy felt him take everything that was in her heart; there was nothing to hold back any more. His soft, deep breathing seemed to drink her up entirely, to take away all that was timid, uncertain, bewildered. Something beautiful and serene came from his heart into hers; wisdom and sadness. If he took her secret, he gave her his in return; that he had renounced life. Nobody would ever share his life again. But he had unclouded faith in the old and lovely dreams of man; that he would teach her and share with her. When they went into the music room, neither of them had spoken.

The tea things were set out before the fire. The kettle had almost boiled dry, and Sebastian went to fill it, leaving Lucy alone in a room which she seemed unable to enter. The piano and the book-shelves were far away, out of reach; and she was far away from herself. She felt as if everything were on the point of vanishing. Now that he knew, he might think it his duty to let her go. He could sweep her existence blank with one word.

He came back, came and stood before her, but she could not look up until she heard her name.

"Don't be frightened, Lucy. I am not going to make love to you. Though it's true enough I love you." He sat down on the arm of her chair. "Why do you crouch away from me like that? And your little hands are so cold. What are you afraid of?"

"I don't know — of things being different. Maybe you won't let me come and play for you any more. Please don't send me away. I won't be a bother."

"Send you away? I'm afraid I'm not so unselfish. Perhaps I ought. But it isn't as if you were really in love. I am quite old enough to be your father, you know. You are merely growing up, — and finding things. It was just that freshness which charmed me, I thought. But now I believe I love everything about you, Lucy. The mornings used to be dull and heavy here. You brought something sweet into them. I began to watch for you from the window, and when I caught sight of you tripping along in the wind, my heart grew lighter. I love young ardour, young fire. I had a nice boy in my house once; but he had to go away to school. What a difference you have made in my life here! When you knocked, it was like springtime coming in at the door. I went to work with more spirit because things were new and wonderful to you."

Lucy pressed her face against his shoulder to hide the tears of happiness. When she heard him tell her that she had given him something!—and only a little while ago that had seemed the most extravagant of all hopes, so foolish that she was ashamed of it, even in the dark. Lying there she felt herself drifting again into his breathing, into his heart-beats. She knew this could not last; in a moment she must gather herself up and be herself again. Yet she knew, too, that it would last a lifetime.

There was a light, familiar knock at the door. She drew away and went over to the fireplace. Giuseppe always knocked like that before he entered with his latch-key. He stuck his head in and asked whether the Signore was ready to dress.

Sebastian told him to come in and lay his clothes out quickly. "I have a dinner engagement, Lucy, and I shall take you home on the way. Wait here for me a few moments. I shan't be long."

He disappeared with Giuseppe, and Lucy sat down in the chair she had quitted. She sat without stirring, her hands lying open in her lap, listening to the faint noises that came up from the street.

In twenty minutes Sebastian came out in his dinner coat. " Can you change as quickly as that, Lucy? " He was standing before the fire, putting on his white gloves, when a latch-key scratched at the door. It opened, and in walked James Mockford, also in a dinner coat; a silk hat on the back of his head and a cane in his hand. Seeing Lucy, he removed his hat and bowed.

" Come in, Jimmy! Where did you drop from? " Sebastian called jovially. Mockford was already in, and Lucy thought he needed no encouragement. There was something impertinent about the way he entered the room.

" From my lodgings. I'm dining with friends, and I thought you might give me a lift in your cab."

Sebastian laughed, as if he liked his coolness. " Sorry, but I'm afraid you'll have to purchase a cab for yourself tonight. I'm taking Miss Gayheart home. However, if you choose to wait here, I suppose I might come back for you."

" Thanks. I'll wait." Mockford put his overcoat and hat on the piano and limped over to the table, where he began eating the sandwiches that had been meant for tea. He looked into each of the two unused cups and wrinkled his nose. Lucy watched him in amazement. She wondered whether he did use white paint, or a liquid powder, on his face at night. He glanced at Sebastian over his plate of sandwiches.

"Wearing a ribbon, I see?"

"The dinner is given for the Belgian Minister."

This time Lucy thought Sebastian spoke rather frigidly. She noticed a tiny purple knot in his lapel. Giuseppe brought his overcoat.

Mockford finished the sandwiches and wiped his fingers.

"How long shall you be gone?"

"Oh, I can stop for you in twenty minutes or so."

"Will you send the hall porter up for me when you come? I don't care to stand about down there on my bad leg. Good night, Miss Gayheart." He half rose when she got up to go, but dropped back immediately. As she went out, she saw him stretched in the deepest chair, his lame foot on the couch, a cigarette hanging loosely between his lips.

"Mustn't let Mockford get on your nerves," Sebastian told her, as he got into the cab after her and shut the door. He patted Lucy's arm soothingly when she tried to protest. "Oh, my dear, I can read your face like a book! You haven't much skill in dissimulation. Jimmy is rather brassy at times, — fault of his early training. He came out

of the slums, really. Mrs. Sebastian found him for
me. A friend of her father discovered this queer,
talented, tricky boy. He's all right at bottom, but
he's not well. That makes him peevish. Just now
he's fighting with me; for his rights, he says. Some
of his cronies have put it into his head that he
ought to be printed on my programs as ' assisting
artist' instead of accompanist. I won't have it,
and he's sulky."

Lucy wanted to say a great deal, but she only
brought out: " In general, then, you think he's —
loyal?"

Sebastian laughed. " Loyal? As loyal as anyone who plays second fiddle ever is. We mustn't
expect too much ! "

13

Lucy used to be sorry that her birthday came
in March. In Chicago it was the most disagree-
able season of the year; and at home, in Haverford, it was always cheerless enough. The ice on
the Platte had either disappeared or gone rotten,
so there was no skating. The wind never stopped
blowing, and the air was full of dust from the
ploughed fields and sand from the river banks.
But this year March was the happiest month she
had ever known.

Book I

Sebastian was getting up his programs for his April concert tour in the East, and every morning was important. It was much more as if he were really living at the studio now. He kept the place full of flowers and growing plants because he found Lucy liked them. When he opened the door for her, he met her with a kiss. That embrace, often playful but never hurried, seemed to bring them at once into complete understanding: every sound, every silence, had the beauty of intimacy and confidence. The air one breathed in that room was different from any other in the world. Lucy thought there was even a special kind of light there, which kept a soft tint of gold, though the fog was brown and the smoke hung low outside. The weather was consistently bad. The ice cakes ground upon each other in the Lake, rain and wet snow beat down upon the city, high winds strewed the streets with broken umbrellas. But when she reached the Arts Building the elevator took her up into an untroubled climate.

It was at night, when she was quiet and alone, that she got the greatest happiness out of each day — after it had passed! Why this was, she never knew. In the darkness she went over every moment of the morning again. Nothing was lost; not a phrase of a song, not a look on his face or a motion of his hand. In these quiet hours she had time to reflect, and to realize that the few weeks since the 4th of January were longer than the twenty-one years that had gone before. Life, it seemed, could not be measured by years.

It was not that she had been discontented before. She had been happy ever since she first came to Chicago; thought herself fortunate to have escaped from a little town to a city, and to work with a kind and conscientious man like Paul Auerbach. But that time was far away. She began a new life on the night when she first heard Clement Sebastian. Until that night she had played with trifles and make-believes.

Since then she had changed so much in her thoughts, in her ways, even in her looks, that she might wonder she knew herself — except that the changes were all in the direction of becoming more and more herself. She was no longer afraid to like or to dislike anything too much. It was as if she had found some authority for taking what was hers and rejecting what seemed unimportant.

One morning Sebastian brought out an old English song, *She Never Told Her Love*. He sang it over several times, walking up and down and smiling to himself: *But let concealment, like a worm i' the bud, feed on her damask cheek.*

He stopped beside the piano and bent down, bringing his face close to Lucy's.

"It doesn't feed on yours, my dear!"

She started and put her hand quickly to her cheek. " But — why should it? I have nothing to conceal! "

" Nothing? Nothing troubles you? "

" How can you ask me? " She looked up at him in astonishment. " When I live my life out under your eyes every day? "

" Don't you sometimes feel it's a waste, living your life out? "

" Not for me, it isn't. Have we finished? "

" Once again, please."

As Lucy got up from the piano, she drew a long breath. " I've never heard that song before. The words are lovely, too."

Sebastian laughed. " Oh, yes? And there are plenty more where those came from." He went to the bookcase, ran his finger along a row of small red leather volumes, and pulled one out of its place. " Take it along. You'll find the lines of this song, and others. Lots of lovely words." He sometimes used that teasing tone, as if she were a child.

Lucy blushed. She had read it, certainly, and had thought it a rather foolish comedy, where everybody was pretending and nobody was in earnest. Until she began to play for Sebastian she had never known that words had any value aside from their direct meaning.

14

Soon after Sebastian left for his Eastern tour, Lucy got a letter from Harry Gordon: he was coming on for a week of the opera, and she must remember her promise. In those days the New York opera company came to Chicago for several weeks every spring. Last year she had been glad to go to the opera with Harry. But now everything was different: she didn't want to see him, didn't want to be reminded of Haverford or of anything that lay behind her. She was going to the Public Library every day now, to hunt through the newspapers for notices of Sebastian's concerts; that took time. Her life was exactly as she wanted it, and Harry would spoil it. He would manage to prove to her that she had been living in a dream, that she was Lucy Gayheart and had been fooling herself all this while.

In his letter Harry asked where he could meet her. She knew he hated calling for her at the bakery. Sebastian didn't mind waiting in the restaurant downstairs when he came to take her out to dinner, but it annoyed Harry. She sent a note to the hotel where he would be stopping, telling him to meet her at Auerbach's studio on Monday, after her lessons. Auerbach's show studio was used as a reception room, when he was not giving a lesson there. His private office opened behind it. Across the hall was a much bleaker room, with a north light, where Lucy heard the younger pupils, and practised if she had a vacant hour.

On Monday afternoon when Lucy came out from this back studio she found Auerbach himself in the reception room, entertaining Harry Gordon, and they seemed to be getting on very well together. As she crossed the room toward him, she suddenly felt pleased with Harry. He came to meet her with such a jolly smile, fresh and ruddy and well turned-out in his new grey clothes. In a flash she was conscious of the thing she had always liked best in him, the fine physical balance which made him a good dancer and a tireless skater. Paul Auerbach seemed as pleased at their meeting as Lucy was herself. He was plainly reluctant to have Harry's call cut short, urged him to come in again, suggested that Lucy bring him out to his house to see Mrs. Auerbach.

As he walked to the door with them, he asked Harry when he had arrived. Harry replied that he had come in " by the morning train," without betraying the fact that he had already been in Chicago three days. He had written his tailor to have two suits ready for the last fitting, and he made no calls until these were sent to his hotel. He wanted to wear exactly what well-dressed men in Chicago were wearing.

After they left the studio, Harry said they must go somewhere for dinner. " Shall we go early, or do you want to dress and have me call for you later?"

" Oh, no! We can dine in state tomorrow evening, before the opera. I'd rather you took me to some quiet place where we can talk."

"Anything you like. We mean to have one good time this week, don't we, Lucy?"

Lucy remembered that when Harry was out for a good time he swept one along with him, just as he did in a polka or a schottish. She liked to do those rather violent, jumpy dances with him; he had a good sense of rhythm and put so much lift and spring behind his partner.

When she got home that evening, Lucy told herself that it was nice to see Harry again. She hated the idea of throwing over old friends. She was thinking, as she undressed, that Harry would be very intelligent if he were not so conceited; it was a kind of mental near-sightedness, and kept him from seeing what didn't immediately concern him. But tonight she hadn't minded that he was pleased with himself, because he was pleased with everything. He hadn't made the countryman's mistake of finding fault with the service and the food. He had tipped the waiters generously, without fumbling or ostentation. He had insisted upon a drive along Michigan Avenue before they came home — a hopeful sign! With the Gordons, who had good horses and carriages of their own, a hired carriage was regarded as a painful extravagance and meant the shortest route. She thought she must have forgotten how much she liked to hear Harry talk — for his voice, chiefly. No matter what he was saying, you could guess his real feeling from his voice, once you knew its several disguises. There was the genial, confidential tone, just tinged by regret, with which he refused a loan to a man who needed it. And there was the other friendliness, not so very different (a little less concerned, indeed), but that was real.

The next evening, for *Aida,* Harry appeared in his new dress clothes, very handsome and correct. Lucy had been teaching all afternoon and was rather tired when they drove to his hotel for dinner, but his good spirits revived her. At the opera they had excellent seats; Harry had written for them weeks ago. He was in his most engaging mood, and didn't once try to ridicule things which she " held sentimentally sacred," as he said. He enjoyed the music, and the audience, and being with Lucy. His enthusiasm for the tenor was sincere; the duet in the third act was, he whispered, his idea of music. He beat time softly to the triumphal march, and didn't mind that the trumpets played off pitch.

When he said good-night to Lucy at the foot of her staircase, she could honestly tell him that she loved going to the opera with him.

15

On the morning after they heard *Otello*, Lucy cut out her practising because Harry had asked her to take him through the Art Museum. It was a rather gentle, sunny morning, and as they walked over toward Michigan Avenue they stopped to do a little shopping. Lucy caught at every pretext for delay. Last year when they went through the Museum together they had disagreed violently about almost everything, and had come away in a bad humour. Marshall Field's was a much better place for Harry, and it was fun choosing handkerchiefs and neckties for him. But he kept looking at his watch, and got her to the galleries soon after they were open. He was careful not to make any comments that would irritate her; she could actually feel caution in his step and voice. What a fury she must have been last spring! Not once did she catch that smart squint in his eyes. He did, occasionally, square his shoulders before a picture and twist his mouth awry, as if he would like to call the painter's bluff; but he did not try to be funny. When they reached a loan exhibit of French Impressionists he broke down, and began pointing out figures that were not correctly drawn.

" Now, you'll admit, Lucy——" he would begin persuasively.

" Certainly I admit, but I don't think it matters. I don't know anything about pictures, but I think some are meant to represent objects, and others are meant to express a kind of feeling merely, and then accuracy doesn't matter."

" But anatomy is a fact," he insisted, " and facts are at the bottom of everything."

She did not answer him impatiently, as she would have done once, but bent her head a little and spoke in a quiet voice which disconcerted him. " Are they, Harry? I'm not so sure."

He didn't reply to this. Something in her tone had made him feel very tenderly toward her. She must be tired, he thought. He saw a door open, leading to one of the stone porticos at the back of the building, that looked on the Lake. He touched Lucy's elbow.

"Let's go out on that balcony and get some fresh air."

The morning had grown warmer, but a mist had come up which hid the sky-line. The water was faintly blue, and above it everything was soft; a silvery mist with changing blue and green at the heart of it, far out. Even the grey gulls flew by on languid wings. The air felt full of spring showers. On a morning like this . . . Lucy felt an ache come up in her throat. When she looked off at that soft promise of spring, spring already happening in the colours of the sky before it had come on earth, such a longing awoke in her that it seemed as if it would break her heart. That happiness she had so lately found, where was it? Everything threatened it, the way of the world was against it. It had escaped her. She had lost it as one can lose a ravishing melody, remembering the mood of it, the kind of joy it gave, but unable to recall precisely the air itself. And she couldn't breathe in this other kind of life. It stifled her, woke in her a frantic fear — the fear of falling back into it forever. If only one could lose one's life and one's body and be nothing but one's desire; if the rest could melt away, and that could float with the gulls, out yonder where the blue and green were changing!

A far-away voice was saying something about lunch. She came back with a start.

" No, Harry, please. I have a headache, and I want to get home as quickly as I can. If I am to go with you tonight, I must lie down and try to get over this."

All that afternoon Lucy stayed quietly in her room. She told herself that she would see Harry Gordon's vacation through and do her best for him. There shouldn't be one flash of temper to regret afterwards. It wasn't his fault that she had changed so much. She was sorry now that she had ever let him come at all, but she must make the best of it. She had enjoyed going to four operas, one right after another. She hadn't heard a great many in her life; she was too busy and too poor. They had listened like two young people who had good seats and who were there to be pleased with everything. Tonight they would hear *Traviata*, and for tomorrow, Saturday, they had chosen the matinée instead of the evening performance, because Lucy had never heard *Lohengrin*, and she especially wanted to.

16

Saturday was a windy, bright April day. There were boys on the streets selling violets and daffodils, and all the barrel-organs were out playing

O Sole Mio! Lucy was in high spirits and felt sure of a happy ending — Harry was leaving to-morrow.

It chanced that Lucy had never heard even the prelude to *Lohengrin* played by an orchestra; the first measures caught her unaware. Before the first act was half over she was longing to be alone; this wasn't the kind of opera to be hearing with Harry. She found herself leaning away from him as far as possible. The music kept bringing back things she used to feel in Sebastian's studio; belief in an invisible, inviolable world. When the act closed and the lights were turned on, her eyes were still shining with tears. If Harry had begun to tease, it wouldn't have mattered then. But he didn't. He glanced sidewise at her and then read his program. Presently he ventured a remark.

"That tenor's fine, now isn't he? He's a good actor, too."

"Yes, he believes in it." She spoke quietly. She was beginning to feel hostile toward him, though he was behaving so well. Harry understood that she was deeply moved. He would have thought that sort of thing ridiculous in a man, but in a girl it was rather attractive.

When the curtain fell on the second act Lucy turned in her seat and looked restlessly about her.

Book I

In the same row, far to the left, a man was leaning forward, looking at her; a red face, a very white shirt-front, an excited, perspiring smile. She caught her breath and cried aloud: " Giuseppe! " though he was not near enough to hear her. She leaned forward and waved her hand. He bowed again and again, in a way that was not familiar, not servile, but wholly devoted and respectful.

The sight of him had brought a rush of delight over her whole body. She shivered and her hands grew cold. That he should have been there all the while, he who was such a part of her other life! She sat through the rest of the opera feeling that nothing had really vanished, everything would come back. When the singers came out to take their curtain calls, she looked not at them but at Giuseppe, who stood applauding with his hands far out in front of him. The ends of his black-and-white silk muffler hung almost to his knees. As the steel curtain descended, he snatched his hat and overcoat and ran off through the crowd. Lucy slipped her arms into the cloak Harry had been patiently holding.

" Who's your enthusiastic friend? " he asked good-naturedly as he steered her toward the back of the house.

" He's an Italian who works about the studio where I go to play accompaniments."

"Music student, you mean?"

"Oh, no! He's just a—workman. But he's very musical."

Harry laughed. "He looks it!"

As they made their way slowly through the crowded foyer, Harry kept trying to hum Lohengrin's farewell to the swan. Lucy began talking rapidly to divert his attention. But Harry had liked that song, and he kept trying! When they stepped outside into the treacherous mildness of the April afternoon, he hailed a cab.

"How about a little drive to get some air? It's too early for dinner. Take us out through the parks, driver, for an hour or so. There's no place anybody can make a call on you, except in a cab, Lucy." He sat down beside her, stretched his long legs, and began to laugh softly. "You know there was something cute about that little dago. I like to see people have a good time. But how the mischief can he afford a seat like that?" He spoke with concern, seemed worried about it.

"Oh, when they admire anything very much, they don't count the cost!" She tried to say this carelessly.

He shook his head. "All the same, the day of counting costs comes along in the end, Lucy mio."

Lucy bit her lip. Wasn't that Harry Gordon in two words! He had been hearing Italian operas all week, and felt acclimated. Lucy mio! And a moment ago he thought he was humming the tenor's aria. She looked out of the window and tried to fix her attention on the misty blue spring sky and the dove-coloured water. Distant light-houses were faintly shining.

Harry didn't mind her silence. He was think-ing he would bring Lucy on for the opera every year. But they might just as well go through to New York; then they could go in mid-winter, when business was dull at home. He was full of his own plans, and the future looked bright to him. There was a part of himself that Harry was ashamed to live out in the open (he hated a sentimental man), but he could live it through Lucy. She would be his excuse for doing a great many pleasant things he wouldn't do on his own account. He pressed her arm as he lounged back in the cab, and began humming the swan song again.

Lucy stirred. " No, it goes like this, Harry."

He ducked his head and laughed. " Right you are! Now suppose we turn and drive back for dinner."

The dining-room at the Auditorium hotel was filling up when they entered. A great many people were dining there before the evening perform-ance. Harry found a table to his taste and ordered champagne to be brought with the soup, remark-

ing that it was never too early for a good thing
" When I have a place of my own, I shall keep
plenty of it on hand — for special occasions."

He talked a good deal through dinner, said
he hated going home tomorrow, but he had to
relieve his father in the bank. His father wanted
to get down to Hot Springs for his rheumatism.
He thanked Lucy for having given him so much
of her time. " Music doesn't mean much to me
without you, except to remind me of you."

She threw him a smile. She had less colour than
usual. She was dreadfully tired. Thank God tonight was the end of it! She had gone her limit,
and now she wanted to be left alone with her own
life.

The dinner seemed to be dragging on, even
the dessert didn't end it. Harry ordered liqueurs
and lit a cigar. He leaned across the table and
took up Lucy's gloves, which were lying by her
plate.

" And now, Lucy—" Something affectionate
and masterful in his voice made her dread what
was coming. " And now isn't it about time we got
down to business? We know each other pretty
well. You've had your little fling. You want to see
the world, but you'll see it a lot better with me.
Why waste any more time? This is April; I should
think we might be married in May. Oh, June if

you like! But we mustn't let another summer slip by."

Lucy frowned and avoided his eyes. "Nonsense, Harry. I'm not ready to marry anyone. I won't be, for a long while."

He put his open palm down heavily on the table. "But I am! Just ready. And we've always known we would do it some day, both of us."

She gave a dry laugh. "Have we? Why, you haven't been sure of yourself half the time!"

Harry chuckled guiltily. "Most of the time I've been sure." Then he looked at her with a singular straightforwardness, looked quite through the professional geniality which usually gleamed over his eyes like a pair of spectacles. "All the time I've been sure at bottom. I have never been able to believe in any sort of happy life except with you. That's the truth."

Lucy felt it was the truth. She could find nothing to say.

"Everything will be just as you wish it. You shall have the kind of house you like, and the kind of friends. I want the life you'd naturally make for yourself, — and it's the only life I do want."

She was trapped. He was looking straight and talking straight. When he was like this she was afraid of him. It seemed unfair to sit there and let him take off all his jocular masks and show

her a naked man who had perhaps never been
exposed to any eye before. She must stop him
before he went any further. She thrust out her
hands across the table.

"Don't, Harry, please! It's no use. Everything
has changed this winter. My life is tied up with
somebody else. It's done. I have no choice. I love
another man."

Gordon seemed not to understand her at first.

"But — what's all this? Another man? And he
lets you play about with me all week? You're
trying to fool me, Lucy!" He looked at her with
a threat in his eyes.

She had fallen into this; she must get out of it,
get it over. "No, I'm not. He's away. It's the
man I work for, play accompaniments for. I'm
not the same person I used to be. I didn't mean
to tell anyone, but I can't let you go on making
plans."

While she was speaking, the harshness on Gordon's face slowly melted. A twinkle came in his
eyes, as if he had found the catch in the puzzle.
He so far forgot himself that he put his hand
down over Lucy's and held it firmly when she tried
to draw it away.

"Now, Lucy! Every girl falls in love with her
singing teacher, but I thought you, for one, had
escaped!"

She felt her cheeks burn with anger. " He's not my singing teacher! He's a great artist," she muttered, angrier still because this sounded so childish.

" Very well, I've no objection; the greater the better! But you'll soon recover, my dear." He refused to be annoyed. He was glowing with tolerance. She gave him a defiant look and managed to get her hand away. He considered a moment, then leaned forward and spoke softly, in a confident, teasing tone. " Now see here, Lucy, how far has this nonsense gone?"

The dining-room swam and tilted before Lucy's eyes. " How far?" she broke out in a flash of scorn. " How far? All the way; all the way! There's no going back. Can't you understand *anything*?" She did not see his face, her eyes were blind as if she were looking into a furnace. But she knew that he got up and left the table.

When she had recovered herself a little, she saw him at the other end of the room, talking to the head waiter. He put something in the waiter's hand and walked out of the dining-room.

Lucy drank some ice-water slowly. She was ashamed that she had lied. She had tried to tell him the truth about a feeling; but a feeling meant nothing to him, he had to be clubbed by a situation. She supposed it was just his coarse good-nature, his readiness to accept as a negligible truancy any thing not actually compromising, that had driven her beyond herself. It was as if he had brought all his physical force, his big well-kept body, to ridicule something that had no body, that was a faith, an ardour. — Why had she ever tried to be nice to him, when she knew all the while he was like that? Well, it was over now, and she hoped she had cut through his stupidity and conceit. It seemed that she had, since he did not come back.

After about a quarter of an hour the head waiter came to her table and, bending down, spoke to her in a way which made an awkward situation seem quite usual and in order.

"Mr. Gordon said, miss, that if he were not back from the telephone in ten minutes, you should not wait for him. He said you would understand."

"Yes, thank you." Lucy caught up her gloves, and her bag, in which there was no money at all. "The check?" she stammered.

"The check is paid, miss. Shall I call a cab for you?"

"Yes, please."

He gave an order to one of the service boys, and held her cloak for her. "You will find it very warm outside, miss, like a summer evening. We have had good weather for the opera season; and last year it was so bad!" He spoke without an accent, but his voice and intonation were unmistakably Italian. He took Lucy through the long dining-room with an air of authority, as if he were conducting some important personage, and at the door motioned one of his subordinates to put her into her carriage. She had not even a quarter to give the boy who brought the cab. Harry Gordon had walked off like that, leaving her to get home as best she could. What a coward, what a boor! She had some money at home, in her bureau drawer; but suppose she didn't have? She might walk home for all he cared.

When the cab stopped before the bakery, she asked the cabman whether he could come upstairs for his fare. "I'm too tired to bring it down, driver."

"Sure, miss. I got a weight. Just sit still while I fasten my hitch-strap." He helped her up the two flights and thanked her for his tip.

17

The next morning Lucy awoke sick and sore. She wanted not to be alone for a moment, and hurried over to Auerbach's studio — perhaps he would have time to give her a lesson.

He met her with a newspaper in his hand. "Look at this, Lucy; Clement is advertised to give a second recital in New York on the 3rd of May. He will scarcely get here before he goes back again. Remarkable success he has had."

That was the important thing. She felt better at once; nothing else mattered, when all was going well with Sebastian. Auerbach himself seemed more wide awake than usual; and for the next few days he gave Lucy the kind of attention and criticism he was usually too easy-going to give any-one. Under his heavy domesticity and middle-aged content there was a discriminating musical intel-ligence—not often brought to the front. As for Lucy, she was working to forget something. But at odd moments that sickening last scene with Harry Gordon would come back upon her and make her angry and ashamed. She hadn't lied often in her life, she was too proud. And that was such a cheap, crawling, shabby lie! It was like boasting she had a claim on Sebastian, when she had none. She had used his name in a way that she could never tell him, and her ears burned when-ever she thought of it. How could she have said such a thing? She considered writing to Harry, but that was difficult. She composed letters to him when she should have been asleep, and the next day put off writing them.

One evening when she went downstairs to get her dinner, she found Giuseppe walking up and down outside, in front of the open stairway. He was wearing a black coat and looked small and grave and important. Off went his hat, and as he stood bareheaded, he broke into such a rush of speech that she could not understand him at all; she caught only that Signor Weisbourn had come to the studio about something urgent. She held up her hand and begged him to speak slowly.

"*Scusi, signorina.*" He put on his hat and began again. Sebastian had written Mr. Weisbourn that all his plans were changed. He had accepted some engagements in England and would sail on the 4th of May, the day after his second New York recital.

Here Lucy interrupted. "But this is the last week of April, Giuseppe. Isn't he coming back here at all?"

"*Si, signorina,* for three days." Sebastian would arrive tomorrow, Friday, and would leave Chicago on Monday night. Giuseppe was to sail with him and would be with him until the engagements in England were over. Then he was going to Italy to see his father. He had been packing all day, to close the studio for the summer. Mr. Weisbourn had not asked him to communicate with Lucy; he had come on his own responsibility, thinking she might have arrangements to make or plans to change.

"No, there is nothing to arrange, Giuseppe. I have no plans. I wish I were going with you."

"And I, signorina, just as we were! It will be like that again when we come back in October. A summer is soon gone."

Lucy could not let Giuseppe go away; not until she had grown a little used to the news he brought, until she had time to take it in. She walked him round and round the block, asking him trivial questions about his preparations, his packing— was the piano gone? No, he had received no orders about the piano.

It was the crowded hour in the crowded part of the city, everyone going home from work. She and Giuseppe could scarcely hear each other speak for the clatter of truck wheels on the dirty pavements. Troops of screaming children on roller skates came streaking down the sidewalk, but Lucy hardly noticed them. She tried to keep close to Giuseppe, and everything around them was blank. An enormous emptiness had opened on all sides of her. This well-disposed little man seemed to be the only person who had thought of her at all. Even he, in his mind, was already outward bound. He began to tell her about the boat, *Wilhelm der Grosse,* on which they were to sail; its length, its tonnage, how many passengers it carried. He would be with the maestro in England and then

they would go to France: before he started for
Florence he would see the maestro's house at
Chantilly, and his dogs, and the Signora Sebastian,
who was the daughter of a mi-lord, did Lucy
know?

As they came round the corner of the block
after many circlings, Lucy felt too tired to hear
any more, and was glad to say good-night. She
forgot to thank him for coming. She did not go
in for dinner, but went languidly upstairs to her
room.

So there would be no return; only another departure. Just now she wished she had never met
Sebastian at all. It would have been better only
to have heard him, to have seen him at a distance,
and to carry away a memory unclouded by personal disappointments. There was nothing sure
or safe in this life she was leading. She had been
sailing along in the air, like a little boy's kite; the
wind drops, and the kite comes down in the dirty
street, among the drays and roller skates.

There had been that one month, to be sure,
when she lived under a golden canopy among
spring flowers, while the March winds and rain
threatened outside the windows. Then she was
never afraid of cruel surprises. Perhaps that was
all she was to have in this world; some people got
very little. It was strange, to feel everything slip-

ping away from one and to have no power to
struggle, no right to complain. One had to sit with
folded hands and see it all go. You couldn't, after
all, live above your level: with good luck you
might, for a few breaths, hold yourself up in that
more vital air, but you dropped back; down, down
into flatness, and it was worse than if you had
never been out of it. She had known that he was
to sail in June — but that had seemed years away.
She had never thought about it for more than a
moment. She hadn't taken it in that after he went
the days and hours would no longer carry her anywhere.

On Saturday morning Lucy was sitting in Sebastian's studio. Both Sebastian and Auerbach
were there; they had been in consultation for some
time before Lucy was sent for. They were talking
to her, about her, around her. Sometimes she listened and sometimes she did not. Finding Auerbach there had made her indifferent to everything.

She had known one of these men so long and
the other so intimately — and now she seemed a
stranger to both. She felt as if she were applying
for a position of some sort, and not very likely to
get it. Moreover, she didn't want it, whatever
it was. She had not the faintest stirring of any

wish or desire; and she did not believe in anything they were saying.

The first shock came when she was told that Sebastian would not be in Chicago next winter, but in New York. Lucy, they said, was to go on in November, and work with him there as she had done here. He and Auerbach had decided that she must stay in Chicago this summer, to study in preparation for next season. Auerbach himself was not going away; he was economizing in order to take his family abroad next year. This studio was leased until October, the rent paid. Sebastian suggested that she move into it as soon as he left it; it would be much cooler than the place where she was living.

Lucy had been listening to them without comment, but now she spoke.

"No, I couldn't leave my own room, Mr. Sebastian. I'm used to it, and I feel at home there."

"But you would get the Lake breezes here. Chicago is very hot, you know. And you would soon feel at home — if you don't already!"

She shook her head. "No, I couldn't do that. I wouldn't feel like myself, moving in here."

Auerbach began to reason with her, but Sebastian cut him short. "No, Paul, we mustn't press it. You'll surely be willing to use this place as a

studio, Lucy? You won't leave a good piano standing here idle? "

Yes, she would be glad to work at his piano.
" But I must have a little time to think about these
things."

" We haven't a great deal of time, Lucy. I
don't like to go away leaving you up in the air.
This isn't the summer for you to go into the country and vegetate. We want you to prepare seriously for next season. Paul understands what I
think you need most, and he has promised to give
you a great deal of attention."

At this point Auerbach rose to go. He stood
holding his hat for a moment, smiling down at the
girl's discouraged face.

" I think you'll let Clement persuade you, Lucy.
A winter in New York would be a fine thing for
you. Then maybe in the spring you can go over to
Vienna with my family. My wife has often said
how she wished you could go with us." The two
men went out to the elevator. They were still
talking about her, Lucy knew. She wished they
would both go away and leave her here to cry.
Everything they wanted her to do seemed out of
her reach.

Sebastian came back and stood over her where
she sat limp in a corner of the sofa.

" Oh, what a morning! First, Paul is so slow to

see things; and then Lucy so unwilling to see things. Why aren't you just a little pleased? Don't you want to play for me any more? Or are you so fond of Chicago you can't leave it?"

"Next winter is a long time away." Lucy looked up and smiled. She was feeling more pleased already. "And May was very near. I guess I'm disappointed to lose it."

"Oh, May would have been dragging out preparations that can be made in two days! Your summer was really the first thing to arrange. Next season is going to be an important one for me. For you, too, I hope. A winter in New York, at your age — you don't know what is waiting for you! And you'll like working with my new accompanist."

"Then Mr. Mockford — ?"

"Is not coming back." Sebastian went over to his writing-desk and began hunting for something, speaking to her over his shoulder. "He doesn't know it yet. We shall arrange all that in England. I intend to see that he's well placed, but he has been with me too long. He and Weisbourn have been putting up some pretty little tricks on me. So I am going to have a new agent and a new accompanist. The best thing about this concert tour has been a revival of interest, in here, I mean," he tapped his chest. "I've met so many old friends who are still interested. Those things are conta-

gious." He put a letter in his pocket and came back
to the sofa. "Ah, now you are looking like Lucy
again! You are beginning to believe in all these
nice things I've thought out for you?"

"No, I wasn't thinking about them. I was
thinking about you. It seems to me that something
good has happened to you."

"Dear child!" For the first time after this
long absence he gathered her up in his arms.
"Now something good has happened to me!
And something good has come back to me."

18

On the last evening Lucy got to the Arts Building just as James Mockford was arriving in a cab,
followed by an express cart. Besides his travelling
luggage, he brought with him a rusty little tin
trunk and a large lounge chair, which he asked
Sebastian to store, as he was giving up his lodgings. Mockford's entrance caused some confusion.
Giuseppe dragged the trunk back into the bedroom, beckoning Lucy to follow him. He whispered to her that later he would get the ugly chair
out of the way, so that she would not have to look
at it. He meant to leave the music room very nice
for her, not like a second-hand shop. She had no-

ticed before that Giuseppe disliked Mockford. He once said to her, when Sebastian's favourite cigarette-case was not to be found, that, since he was responsible for the place, no one but he should have a latch-key, *no one!* — with a murderous flash in his quick eyes.

After Morris Weisbourn had arrived, and they were all gathered in the music room, Mockford was the only person altogether cheerful. He was so pleased to be leaving Chicago that he made himself agreeable even to Lucy. Sebastian was at the bookcase behind the piano, going over a pile of music. Giuseppe, who had been so delighted to be starting for home, and to be sailing on a big boat, had lost his enthusiasm. He stood in the background among the trunks, his hands crossed before him, solemn and hushed, as if he were waiting for a coffin to be carried out. They were all, of course, impatiently expecting the transfer men who were to come and get the luggage. The air in the room was heavy and hot — no breeze, though all the windows were open. Out over the Lake the sky was black, and from time to time there was a low growl of thunder.

Sebastian called Lucy to his corner and began giving her some directions, to which she tried to listen. But she was distracted by Weisbourn and Mockford, who were talking very loud, as if they wished everything they said to be heard. They had seated themselves by an open window and were finishing the last bottle of port. Weisbourn must have been drinking before he came; his dark blue cheeks looked very thick, and his eyes were small. The moment they sat down together they had been overtaken by the brotherly affection which beams from two schemers who have done each other a good turn.

"And when you are to be operate, you will send me a cable? So?"

Sebastian shot a glance of amusement at the two from behind the piano. Lucy saw their wineglasses touch, one in the round fat hand, the other in the white freckled one.

Just then came heavy sounds and knocking at the door. Giuseppe flew to admit the baggage men. "Thank God!" Sebastian murmured. As soon as the trunks had gone down, he put on his topcoat and turned to Mockford and Weisbourn.

"Gentlemen, I have some calls to make, and I am going to take Miss Gayheart home. I shan't be back here. I will meet you at the station. Giuseppe will take the hand luggage down at eleven. Leave the keys with the doorman."

The cab Sebastian customarily used had been waiting outside half an hour. He told the driver to open the windows and take them out to the Park.

"You are worn out with all the fuss, and so am I," he said as they drove up the avenue. He drew her head over on his shoulder. "There. Shut your eyes and rest. We have three hours, all our own." He felt her soft young body take the line of his as she lay against him. She breathed lightly, like a child sleeping. He, too, closed his eyes. The warm night air blew in over their faces. After a while it began to smell of trees and new-cut grass, and the confused city noises died away.

Sebastian felt a wet splash on his face. He put his hand out of the window; it was raining a little. Then it came down harder, a fierce spring shower.

"Asleep, Lucy?"

"No."

"We were glad to get away, weren't we? But I've grown fond of that studio. I like to think it's not going to be shut up dumb and dusty all summer, that you'll be coming and going. I shall be thinking of you. When I am at sea, I shall look at my watch every morning and figure the difference in time and tell myself whether you have opened the piano yet."

Lucy buried her face closer, her hand on his shoulder tightened. She felt the tears rising and could not hold them back.

"I ought to do better than this. I'm so sorry!" she quavered.

" Never mind, dear. Cry if you feel like it. Perhaps I shall cry with you."

" It's only because I'm so afraid."

" Afraid again? Of what? "

" Oh, that you'll never come back! Something tells me you won't."

" That's because you are just beginning, and are not used to good-byes. They hurt, sometimes, even after one has gone through a great many." Sebastian felt a heaviness of heart; he scarcely knew whether on her account or his own. He was wondering whether there was not some way of escape from his life: from concerts and hotels, from Mockford, and his wife, and his place in France, from his friends in England, from everything he was and had. In what stretched out before him there was nothing he wanted very much. And this youth and devotion would not be the same when he came back, he knew; what he held against his heart was for tonight only. It was a parting between two who would never meet again.

Lucy knew what he was thinking. She felt a kind of hopeless despair in the embrace that tightened about her. As they passed a lamppost she looked up and in the flash of light she saw his face. Oh, then it came back to her! The night he sang *When We Two Parted* and she knew he had done something to her life. Presentiments

like that one were not meaningless; they came
out of the future. *Surely that hour foretold sorrow to this.* They were going to lose something.
They were both clinging to it and to each other,
but they must lose it.

Presently Sebastian stopped the carriage and
told the driver he could wait for them. He took
Lucy's arm and they walked for a long while up
and down the winding gravel paths, the bitter
fragrance of young lilac leaves coming sharp
into their faces at every turn. The rain had
stopped, but the dripping bushes showered them
with waterdrops. Their hands and faces were
wet; it was good to feel. There was not a star to
be seen, but the blackness above them was soft
and velvety between the scattered park lights.
Sebastian was telling Lucy that perhaps next summer they would be walking under night skies far
away from here. If she went abroad with the
Auerbachs, he would join them in Vienna. There
were a great many things he would like to show
her for the first time; gardens — forests —
mountains.

They had turned back toward the carriage, the
wet gravel crushing softly under their feet. As he
came under one of the lamp-posts, he slipped out
his watch. He said nothing to Lucy, but he gave
the cabman her street-number. They drove back

into the heart of the city in silence, as they had
come away from it.

At the bakery entrance Sebastian got out and
followed Lucy up the two flights of stairs to her
own door. In the dim hall light he took her face in
his hands and looked into it for a long moment.
Lucy felt the old terror coming back; *to sever for
years.* . . . She couldn't bear it any longer.

" Go," she whispered, " go now ! " She scarcely
felt his arms, his lips; she could only think that
in a moment he would not be there at all. He held
her closer and closer, and then he let her go. She
stood just inside her door, leaning against it, listening to his quick heavy tread down the first stairway — the second — then she heard the cab door
slam.

Sebastian knew she was listening. He shut the
door violently to end her suspense. A last signal.
He sank back in the seat and closed his eyes as the
cab lumbered off. Against the rumble of the wheels
he spoke aloud to himself. What he said was:

" *Ein schöner Stern ging auf in meiner Nacht.*"

19

One hot morning in the middle of May, Lucy
was putting fresh lavender bags in her bureau
drawers. Lifting a pile of muslin underclothes,

she came upon an unopened letter — a letter from Haverford, from Pauline! She laughed, but she was ashamed, really! It had come a week ago, when she was just beginning to practise in Sebastian's studio, trying to feel at her ease there, and she was afraid of anything that might dishearten her. Pauline's letters often had that effect, so she tucked this one out of sight for the moment, — and then forgot all about it. She thought, as she took it up and looked at it, that perhaps she hadn't made a mistake in forgetting! The letter was thick and bulky (a bad sign), and the handwriting on the envelope looked, even more than usual, like eggs rolling downhill. Pauline had inherited so many German characteristics — what a pity she couldn't have inherited a German script!

As Lucy opened the letter some newspaper clippings fell out. Pauline announced the theme at once. Harry Gordon was married! Married to Miss Arkwright of St. Joe, and they had started for Alaska on their wedding trip. Everyone in Haverford was "talking." People thought he had treated Lucy very badly. It was a great shock to her old friends. They had always believed his "intentions" were serious. They were asking Pauline what had happened, and she didn't know what to say. What did Lucy wish her to say, "under the circumstances"?

Lucy tore the letter to bits and threw it into the

waste-basket. So Harry thought he would show her, did he? Such haste must have inconvenienced Miss Arkwright a trifle; but that wouldn't bother Harry, if he had his revenge. He must have given her about a week's notice! The announcement in the *St. Joseph Gazette* said they were to live in Haverford! That would certainly be dull for the bride. She crumpled the clipping and threw it after the letter.

" It would be a joke," she said to herself, " if Harry has gone and married Miss Arkwright more on my account than her own."

She laughed, but all the same that announcement left a bitter taste in her mouth. As she got ready to walk over to the studio, she was thinking that she had lost an old friend; and she had told him the kind of falsehood that made her think poorly of herself.

When she reached the Arts Building the hall porter's smile, hand to cap, changed the colour of her thoughts. George, the elevator man, held his car back to tell her there was a storm on its way from Duluth. The attendants about the place were devoted to Sebastian, and they admired Lucy. That was pleasant. They liked to see her come and go; so many of the studios were empty now.

Lucy hung her hat and jacket exactly where she used to put her winter things. Giuseppe had left one of Sebastian's rain-coats hanging in the entry hall, and a collection of walking-sticks in the rack. She went into the music room, opened the windows, and stood breathing in the fresh air and looking out at the glittering blue water.

She had not begun to come here at once after Sebastian went away, — not, indeed, until she had a note from him, written on the boat and sent back by the tug. He began:

" It is eleven o'clock here. That means that you have just got to the studio and are opening the piano. I shall listen to hear that you do not begin lazily. I still feel more there than here."

An hour after that letter came, she used her latch-key for the first time. Not for a moment had the place seemed forlorn or deserted. To her it was full of the man himself. All her companionship with him was shut up there, and the future was beginning to live there, — the future in which she couldn't help believing. She came here by his wish; the quiet and comfort of the place were his kindness. She was thus lifted up above the sweating city streets because of his concern for her. Those ardent early-summer days, with heat that still had an edge of freshness, were glorious days for work. She had never had such

a piano at her command, or so definite a purpose
to direct her.

The weeks flew by, but Lucy flew faster than
they. The heavy July heat made no drain on her
vitality. This was the first summer she had spent
in the city, and she found it stimulating; no hotter
than Haverford, and God knew how much less
dull! She seemed to be carried along on a rushing
river, and was constantly saluting beautiful things
on the shore. She couldn't stop to see them very
clearly, but they were there, flashing on the right
or the left. And when the morning was over, and
she was tired, she was glad to creep home through
the heat and do her darning or put ribbons in her
nightgowns.

Auerbach had very few pupils in the summer
months, and he gave her a great deal of time. He
liked to have her with him, and urged her to spend
her week-ends with his family. He had a house of
his own out on the South Shore, and a garden.
From the first green of spring, he rose very early
and worked for two hours in his garden before he
went into the city to his classes. His wife got up
and made his breakfast, long before the children
or the housemaid were awake. She told Lucy that
as you got older there wasn't so much you could
do for your husband any more, and it was nice to

give him a good breakfast while you had the house to yourself.

Auerbach inquired after Harry Gordon occasionally. He liked the young man, and he had hopes for Lucy in that direction. She never told him of Harry's marriage. She was hurt, though she pretended to be scornful. He hadn't really a right to marry; he had belonged for years to Lucy Gayheart!

One Sunday morning they were sitting in the shade under Auerbach's grape arbour. Auerbach, in his shirt-sleeves, began to question her.

" I think you have changed your mind, Lucy. You would rather go on with the kind of work you do with Clement than teach? "

As Lucy made no reply, he continued.

" You must remember that Clement is very exceptional. Most singers are not interesting to work with, and they don't want to pay much. For the platform they always have a man."

Still Lucy said nothing. She bit her lip and looked out of the end of the arbour at the yellow squash blossoms. Auerbach smiled.

" Perhaps you have another plan, eh? The big Westerner? That would please me very well."

" You are mistaken, Mr. Auerbach. That is only a friendship."

" Maybe so. But I wouldn't be sorry to see it

come to something else. In the musical profession there are many disappointments. A nice house and garden in a little town, with money enough not to worry, a family — that's the best life."

"You think so because you live in a city. Family life in a little town is pretty deadly. It's being planted in the earth, like one of your carrots there. I'd rather be pulled up and thrown away."

Auerbach shook his head. "No, you wouldn't. I've heard young people talk like that before. You will learn that to live is the first thing."

Lucy asked him if there were not more than one way of living.

"Not for a girl like you, Lucy; you are too kind. Even for women with great talent and great ambition — I don't know. Some have good success, but I don't envy them."

The next morning, when Lucy opened the windows in the studio and looked across at the Lake, she told herself that she wasn't going out to the Auerbachs' any more. It dampened her spirits. He was a heavy, thorough, German music-teacher, and there he stopped.

20

Lucy often spent the long hot evenings in Sebastian's music room, lying on the sofa, with the big windows open and the lights turned out. And how strange it was that she should be there, after all! Only last Christmas, when she went home, she had never been inside this room, and had thought herself fortunate to catch a glimpse of Sebastian coming out of the doorway downstairs.

This summer there would be no slowing-down to the village pace. No walking about the town for hours and hours in the moonlight: down to the post-office and home again; out to the little Lutheran church at the north end. At this hour she used often to be sitting on the church steps, looking up at that far-away moon; everything so still about her, everything so wide awake within her. When she couldn't sit still any longer, there was nothing to do but to hurry along the sidewalks again; diving into black tents of shadow under the motionless, thick-foliaged maple trees, then out into the white moonshine. And always one had to elude people. Harry and the town boys had their place, but on nights like this she liked to be alone. She wondered she hadn't worn a trail in the sidewalks about the Lutheran church and the old high school. She wondered that her heart hadn't burst in those long vacations, when there was no human image she could hold up against the summer night; when she was alone out there, looking up at the moon from the bottom of a well.

She loved her own little town, but it was a heart-breaking love, like loving the dead who cannot answer back.

Now the world seemed wide and free, like the Lake out yonder. She was not always struggling against something, she was going with something much stronger than herself. It was not that this new life was without pain. But there was nothing empty or meaningless in it, nothing that was not sweet to remember; not even that last night when they had walked under the dripping trees and breathed in the bitter darkness together.

From the very beginning there had been the shadow of some sorrow over her love for this man, even before she knew him at all. When she used to get only a glimpse of him now and then, on the street, on the steps of the Art Museum, coming out of the Cathedral, it was the look of loneliness and disappointment in his face that had drawn her heart after him. Now, when he was far away, she sometimes went into the church where the service for Madame de Vignon was held and where she had seen Sebastian pray so long and fervently. It was a place sacred to sorrows she herself had never known; but she knelt in the spot where he had knelt, and prayed for him.

She heard from Sebastian occasionally, short

notes, not love-letters; a few words about his engagements or about her own studies. There was always something meant for her alone; an anecdote, a memory, a sentence about a place which had stirred him — a human word. He kept her informed as to his itinerary, so that she always knew where he was. He had finished his summer's work in Munich, and was going to the Italian lakes for his holiday.

2 1

One morning Mrs. Paul Auerbach came out into the garden and told her husband that his breakfast was ready. It was September, and he was cutting his grapes.

While she was bringing in his coffee he sat down and opened the morning paper. She heard him call to her, and knew by his voice that something terrible had happened. She ran into the dining-room. Paul did not speak, but pointed to the newspaper spread out on the table. Mrs. Auerbach saw the headlines and sank into a chair beside him. Together they read the cablegram from Milan.

Yesterday Clement Sebastian and James Mockford were drowned when their boat capsized in a sudden storm on Lake Como. There were three in the boat, Sebastian, his accompanist, and Gus-

tave Wiertz, the Belgian violinist. The accident
was seen from the shore, and two row-boats immediately put out from Cadenabbia, but only
Wiertz was rescued. His account of the accident
followed:

The breeze had stopped altogether, but they
had not taken down their sail. When the hurricane
from the mountains broke upon them, the boat
was turned over immediately. Wiertz himself was
struck by the boom and thrown out a considerable
distance. He sank, and when he came up saw his
two companions struggling in the water. He felt
no alarm for Sebastian, who was a strong swim-
mer. Mockford could not swim and was appar-
ently terrified; he had locked his arms about
Sebastian's neck. Wiertz thought Sebastian would
be able to control a man so much slighter, so he
swam toward the boats coming out from shore.
The water was so cold that he was already growing numb, and he did not look over his shoulder
again. When he was pulled into the first row-boat,
the two heads had disappeared. The second rescue
party went on, believing that the two men might
be clinging to the overturned sail-boat. But they
found no one. Mockford must have fastened
himself to his companion with a strangle-hold and
dragged him down. The bodies had not yet been
recovered.

Auerbach looked at his watch. "My God, Minna, I must get to poor Lucy before she sees this! It is not seven o'clock yet. I think she never comes downstairs before eight."

"Wait, Papa, wait! I must go, too. I can put on my coat and go like this. Oh, the poor child, the poor child!"

BOOK II

BOOK II

I

It seemed as if the long blue-and-gold autumn in the Platte valley would never end that year. All through November women still went about the town of Haverford in the cloth tailored suits which were the wear in 1902, with perhaps a little fur piece about the throat; no one had thought of putting on a winter coat. The trees that hung over the cement sidewalks still held swarms of golden leaves; the great cottonwoods along the river gleamed white and silver against a blue sky that was just a little softer than in summer. The air itself had a special graciousness. Even people who had some right to grumble that the rainfall had been scant and the corn burned in the tassel, came out into their yards every morning with the feeling that things would be better next year and life was a good gamble.

On such a morning Mrs. Alec Ramsay, widow
of one of the founders of Haverford, was sitting
by the wide window of her front parlour, in her
favourite tapestry winged-chair. She was an old
woman now, quite seventy, though the people of
Haverford could scarcely realize it; she had
been a commanding figure in their lives for so
long. Moreover, she did not look her age; she was
still erect and handsome, there was something
regal in her carriage and manner. Her neighbours
did remark that she had softened with time, had
become more reflective and sympathetic. Ten
years ago she would not have been sitting in a
deeply cushioned chair at nine o'clock in the
morning of a fine autumn day. She would have
been driving into the country, or marketing on
Main Street, or taking the fast train to Omaha
for a day's shopping. She still drove out, or
walked, every afternoon; but in the morning she
was rather quiet, as if she had to husband the
energy that had once been an unfailing source.
And she was more interested in other people, all
people, now than she used to be. This morning
she was looking out of her window to watch
the children go by on their way to school;
little boys in knee-pants and shirt-waists, little
girls in starched gingham dresses. " Run, Molly,
run ! " she called to a little fat one who came

scampering along just as the last bell began to ring.

When the bell stopped, and all the children of the town were safely penned in three red brick schoolhouses, then the older people came along, going to the post-office for their morning mail: Doctor Bridgeman's plump wife, who walked to reduce; Jerry Sleeth, the silent, Seventh-day Advent carpenter; Father MacCormac, the Catholic priest; flighty little Mrs. Jackmann, who sang at funerals — and on every other possible occasion. One after another they came along the sidewalk in front of the house, under the arching elm trees, which were still shaggy with crumpled gold and amethyst leaves.

Suddenly Mrs. Ramsay turned in her chair and spoke to her daughter, Madge Norwall, who had come down from Omaha on a visit. Mrs. Norwall was in the back room of the long double parlour, knitting a sweater for a son in college.

"Madge, there goes Lucy Gayheart. She's so changed, poor child, you'd scarcely know her. She never used to pass without looking in."

The slender girl who was coming down the sidewalk did not glance to right or left, nor could one say that she was looking before her. She was definitely not looking at all, Mrs. Norwall thought. Her head was bent forward a little and her shoulders were drawn together, as if she were trying to slip past unnoticed. Mrs. Ramsay could not let her go by like that; she leaned forward and tapped on the window-pane with her big cameo ring. The girl stopped, flashed a glance at the window, smiled, waved her hand faintly, and hurried on.

Mrs. Ramsay watched the diminishing figure with a wistful, anxious look in her still lovely blue eyes, — a blue that was light and silvery clear, like the blue of sapphires. Lucy had always walked rapidly, but with a difference. It used to be as if she were hurrying toward something delightful, and positively could not tarry. Now it was as if she were running away from something, or walking merely to tire herself out.

Mrs. Norwall had come into the front room and was looking out over her mother's shoulder.

"I wonder what it is," murmured Mrs. Ramsay. "Some people say it was a love-affair in Chicago. And some say it is because she lost her position there. I can't see her taking a thing like that much to heart."

"And still others say," the daughter added, "that it's because Harry Gordon jilted her and married Miss Arkwright."

"No such thing!" Mrs. Ramsay threw her head back with a flash of her old fire. "If there was any jilting done, Lucy did it. He'd have been glad enough to get her. I knew, the moment I saw them together, he'd married this lantern-jawed woman out of pique. Certainly Lucy is much too good for him."

" Harry's a grand business man, and he's very handsome," said Mrs. Norwall teasingly.

" Handsome on the outside, perhaps. I should call it fine-looking, myself. Rough Scotch at heart. I saw plenty of his kind in Scotland; never too proud to save a shilling, for all their swank and bluster."

Mrs. Norwall smiled and went on with her sweater. Mrs. Ramsay looked out of the window and watched the people going by; nodded and smiled if they happened to look in, but she scarcely saw them. Her thoughts were elsewhere. Presently she sighed and said, as if to herself:

"Whatever it was, I wish it hadn't happened. Poor little Lucy ! "

Mrs. Norwall glanced up from her work, almost startled by something beautiful in her mother's voice. It was not the quick, passionate sympathy that used to be there for a sick child or a friend in trouble. No, it was less personal, more ethereal. More like the Divine compassion. And her mother used to be so stormy, *so* personal ! If growing old did that to one's voice and one's understanding, one need not dread it so much, the daughter was thinking.

Lucy Gayheart hurried on with no particular thought in her mind except that she would go home by another way; she would go up Main Street as far as the old high school, and turn west a good four blocks north of Mrs. Ramsay's. She had loved and admired Mrs. Ramsay all her life, and for that reason she couldn't bear to see her now. Once, since she first came home in September, Lucy had stopped at Mrs. Ramsay's house, but it was all she could do to sit through a short call. Her throat closed up, and her mind seemed frozen stiff. Her old friend could not help her — only one person in Haverford could help her. She was going to the post-office now on the chance of seeing him, as she had gone on many another morning. All the business men went for their mail at about half past nine. Suddenly she remembered that the school-bell had rung a long while ago. She might be too late; she hurried faster.

The double doors of the post-office were hooked back because of the warm weather. Men were going in and coming out. Lucy went to her father's box and slowly turned the combination lock about, purposely getting it wrong. She was waiting for someone. In a few moments Harry Gordon came

in. The bank lock-box was a little way beyond
Jacob Gayheart's. He passed behind Lucy without
seeing her, opened his box, and threw the letters
into a leather bag he carried. As he turned to
leave, Lucy stood directly in his way.

" Good morning, Harry."

He looked up, pulled off his hat, and exclaimed:
" Why, *good* morning, Lucy! " As if he were
very much surprised to see her here; as if she had
never been away and never come back; as if there
had never been any special friendship between
them. His voice had just that impersonal cordial-
ity he had with unimportant customers or their
womenfolk. She might have been a girl from one
of the farms on which he held a claim he would
gladly be rid of. And his eyes seemed to look at
her through thick glasses, though he never wore
any. Keen, sparkling, pale blue eyes, as cold as
icicles. He was not stiff with her, — perfectly
casual; and he went out of the post-office and down
the street with that easy, confident stride with
which he used to go out on the diamond in old
baseball days, when he was the best pitcher in the
Platte valley and Lucy was a little girl watching
from the grand-stand.

Again and again since she came back to Haverford they had met like this; and it was always just
the same: the same affectation of surprise, the

same look, the same tone of voice — to one who knew all the shades of his voice so well. If he had been embarrassed or curt, she might have got round it. But there was no breaking through this particular manner of his. Poor farmers couldn't break through it when Harry proposed a settlement little to their advantage and much to his own. He had a natural vigorous heartiness which was as convincing as his fresh complexion. It was so open and unlike the manner of a skinflint, that a slow-witted man couldn't realize he had agreed to a hard bargain until it was over and he was driving home in his wagon.

If she could only get a message to him, Lucy was thinking as she walked away. She wanted little more than a friendly look when he passed her on the street, the sort of look he used to give her, careless and jolly. It would be enough if he would stop on the street-corner occasionally and tell her a funny story in his real voice, which very few people ever heard, and look at her with the real kindness that used to be like a code sign between them whenever they met.

Lucy did not go directly home, though she knew Pauline was waiting for the morning paper. She went up to the north end of town, to the little Lutheran church, and sat down on the steps. It lay higher than the rest of Haverford, at the edge of the open country, and one could look out over the low hills, chequered with brown, furrowed wheat-fields, to the windings of the Platte River. She sat down there because she was tired, and then she forgot to think about the time. The sunlight fell warm on the wooden steps. An osage orange hedge shut out the only house that was near by, and the place was quiet and friendly. Presently she heard a bell, — the school-bell! Then it must be eleven o'clock. She hurried home as fast as she could.

Pauline was in the dining-room, setting the table. Lucy went straight to her.

"I'm sorry I forgot to bring the paper home, Pauline. I went for a walk and was gone longer than I meant to be."

"Oh, that's all right!" said Pauline in the cheery tone which meant that it wasn't right at all.

Lucy put the paper down and went quickly upstairs to her own room. Good heavens, why had she become so sensitive to people's voices! Everyone she met spoke to her in an unnatural, guarded tone. Her father's seemed to be the only honest voice in town.

Pauline called to her that lunch was ready. She came downstairs and took her place at the table, opposite her sister. Mr. Gayheart always lunched in town, at the Bohemian beer saloon. Pauline

brought in a platter of mutton chops; the coffee-
pot and vegetables were already on the table.
"Any important letters?" she asked as she sat
down.

"Important? No." Lucy supposed she must
mean a letter calling her back to Chicago.

Pauline chattered away. As a little girl Lucy had
trained herself to close her mind when her sister
went rambling on. (Even then it had seemed to
her that most women talked too much.) Now, as
then, she tried to keep her mind on something
outside the house. Pauline had a very informal
way of eating when they were alone; neglected
her food to talk, and then gobbled. Lucy couldn't
dismiss things of that kind lightly as she used to.
They chafed her and made her shrink into herself.

Suddenly Pauline came out with something
which she really wanted to say, and then Lucy
heard her.

"There, I nearly forgot after all! Mrs. Ramsay telephoned and said she very particularly
wanted you to come in this evening. She wants just
you, because I was there last week, the day after
Madge came. You know we *all* liked Madge. Can
you realize she has a boy in college this year?"

"Yes, I remember him. We called him Toddy.
His real name was Theodore, wasn't it? I suppose
I'll have to go."

"Of course you will. You were always a special favourite." Pauline gave a generous emphasis to this sentence. And it was generous of her, Lucy admitted; for Mrs. Ramsay had always treated Pauline like Pauline and Lucy like Lucy. But was generosity ever a grace when it came with a pull? Wasn't it like the quality of mercy and the gentle dew? Her sister broke in upon her reverie.

"Lucy, you're not eating anything again! That's why you've lost your colour. You know, it's not becoming to you to be pale. There's a new preparation of cod-liver oil — "

Lucy interrupted her firmly. "Pauline, I took that medicine when I first came home to please you, not because I thought it would do me any good. It doesn't help people to eat when they are not hungry. I worked too hard last summer, and had a kind of nervous smash-up at the end of it. The only thing that will help me is to be alone a great deal. That's why I came home, and why I don't go to see people. That's why I begged you to leave the orchard, too. I didn't lose my job, as some of our friends seem to think. My coming away put Professor Auerbach to a great deal of trouble. But he wouldn't let me try to work when I was sick."

"Well, Lucy," said Pauline as she began gathering up the dishes, "that's the most reasonable ex-

planation of things you've given me yet. Of course
I want to help you to get well. But if you expect
people to help you, you must tell them a little
about what is the matter. And you certainly have
kept us in the dark."

"I know." Lucy spoke contritely, but she drew
closer back within herself and looked at the floor.
"I'm not a very reasonable person. You've had
a good deal to put up with. I think I'm beginning
to get a little steadier."

Pauline had spoken kindly, and she still meant
to be kind when she went on:

"You must be plain and outspoken with your
own folks, Lucy, and not theatrical. We aren't
that kind, and we don't know how to behave."

"Yes, I understand, Pauline." Lucy spoke very
low. She was not angry, but she went upstairs to
her own room without once meeting her sister's
eyes.

A few moments later Pauline saw her go out
of the house carrying an old carriage robe, and
disappear into the apple orchard behind the
garden.

2

All afternoon Lucy lay in the sun under a low-
branching apple tree, on the dry, fawn-coloured

grass. The orchard covered about three acres and sloped uphill. From the far end, where she was lying, Lucy looked down through the rows of knotty, twisted trees. Little red apples still clung to the boughs, and a few withered grey-green leaves. The orchard had been neglected for years, and now the fruit was not worth picking. Through this long, soft, late-lingering autumn Lucy had spent most of her time out here.

There is something comforting to the heart in the shapes of old apple trees that have been left to grow their own way. Out here Lucy could remember and think, and try to realize what had happened to her: remember how the kind Auerbachs had come to her that morning (long ago it seemed) and taken her home with them. Paul had understood, without being told, that she must get away, must go home, that she wished never to see Chicago again.

Mrs. Auerbach did all her packing for her, made explanations to the bakery people, got her railway ticket, took Lucy to the train. She had even made up a little package of " keepsakes " at Sebastian's studio, before his lawyer came in to clean everything out; some of the handkerchiefs left in his drawer, a pair of his gloves, photographs of himself and his friends, a few of his books, scores he had marked. She selected these

things without consulting Lucy and sent them by
express to Haverford. They now lay in the bottom
of Lucy's trunk. They meant nothing to her; she
couldn't bear to look at them.

To have one's heart frozen and one's world
destroyed in a moment — that was what it had
meant. She could not draw a long breath or make
a free movement in the world that was left. She
could breathe only in the world she brought back
through memory. It had been, and it was gone.
When she looked about this house where she had
grown up, she felt so alien that she dreaded to
touch anything. Even in her own bed she lay tense,
on her guard against something that was trying to
snatch away her beautiful memories, to make her
believe they were illusions and had never been
anything else. Only out here in the orchard could
she feel safe. Here those feelings with which she
had once lived came back to her.

Her father's house was accounted comfortable;
she could recall that she used to take pride in it.
But all those wooden dwellings in Western towns
were flimsily built, — built for people without
nerves. The partitions were too thin, especially
between the upstairs chambers. Her own room
was next Pauline's. She could not cry, or switch
on her light, or turn over in bed, without knowing
that her sister heard her.

Out here in the orchard she could even talk to herself; it was a great comfort. She loved to repeat lines from some of Sebastian's songs, trying to get exactly his way of saying the words, his accent, his phrasing. She tried to sing them a little. It made her cry, but it melted the cold about her heart and brought him back to her more than anything else did. Even that first air she ever played for him, "*Oh that I knew . . . . where I might find Him . . .*" she used to sing it over and over, softly, passionately, until she choked with tears. But it helped her to say those things aloud to her heart, as if something of him were still living in this world. In her sleep she sometimes heard him sing again, and both he and she were caught up into an unearthly beauty and joy. "*So shall the righteous shine forth as the sun in their heavenly Father's realm.*" It was like that, when she heard him in her sleep.

But sometimes she was afraid of sleep, and did not go to bed, but sat up in a little chair by the window for hours rather than take that chance. There had been nights when she lost consciousness only to drop into an ice-cold lake and struggle to free a drowning man from a white thing that clung to him. His eyes were always shut as if he were already dead; but the green eyes of the other, behind his shoulder, were open, full of terror and

greed. She awoke from such dreams cold and ex-
hausted with her struggle to break that cowardly
embrace. Then she would lie awake for the rest
of the night, shivering. Why had she never told
Sebastian she knew this man was destined to de-
stroy him? Why hadn't she thrown herself at his
feet and pleaded with him to beware of Mockford, that he was cowardly, envious, treacherous,
and she knew it!

After one of these terrible nights Lucy was
afraid to trust herself with anyone. A very little
thing might shatter her self-control. She would
come out here under the apple trees, cold and
frightened and unsteady, and slowly the fright
would wear away and the hard place in her breast
grow soft. And now the orchard was going to be
cut down; the old trees were feeling the sun for
the last time this fall.

Just behind the orchard was the pasture where
Mr. Gayheart used to graze a horse, in the days
when he kept one. Two years ago Pauline had this
field ploughed up and planted in Spanish onions.
She marketed very profitable crops, and that
sealed the fate of the orchard.

Lucy had been at home only a few weeks when
she was awakened one morning by the sound of an
ax. She listened languidly for a moment, then sud-

denly realized that it wasn't somebody chopping wood. The sound was not like that at all; there was no vibration. The ax was cutting into something alive. She sprang out of bed, caught up a dressing-gown, and ran to her father's big room at the back of the house, which looked out over the yard and the orchard. Her father was in the bathroom, shaving. From his window she could see a man in the orchard, cutting down an apple tree. She ran down the back stairs to the kitchen, where Pauline was getting breakfast, and told her to go out to the orchard, quick! Someone was cutting a tree.

Pauline looked sidewise out of her rather small eyes. Her voice was not quite natural as she tried to answer carelessly.

" I told Poole to come today, but I didn't tell him to come so early. I'm sorry if he wakened you."

" But what's the matter with the tree? Why is he cutting it?"

Pauline broke an egg into the hot saucepan. " Hadn't I told you we are going to clear away the old orchard?"

" Clear away — Oh, where is Father?"

Startled by the frantic note in her sister's voice, Pauline pushed the eggs to the back of the stove and turned round.

"Father has agreed to it. You surely must know, Lucy, that he turns in very little money toward the running of this house. My onion crops have done a good deal for us. I am having the orchard cut down this fall and the ground prepared, so that I can put it into onions and potatoes in the spring. I can't be going out to the farms all the time to look things over, and I'm sure the tenants cheat me. But here I can have a crop under my eyes and make a good thing of it. I have to turn some trick, to keep the place going."

"But, Pauline, don't do it this fall. Don't do it now, when I'm so miserable!"

"Try to be reasonable, Lucy. I've made all the arrangements, and if I put it off I lose a year's crop."

Lucy was still scarcely awake. She caught Pauline's chubby hand and broke out wildly: "I can't stand it, I can't! It's all I have in the world just now. Leave it this year, and I'll pay you back what you lose, truly I will. I'll soon be making money again, and I'll pay you every cent. Pauline, go out and send that man away! Listen, it's down! He'll begin on another. I can't stand it!" Lucy dropped into a chair, and her head sank upon her bare arms on the kitchen table. Her hair was hanging in two braids over her shoulders which were shaking with bitter sobs. Pauline frowned darkly, but her own eyes filled with tears. She couldn't doubt the desperateness of Lucy's distress, and she looked so helpless. Not since she was a child had she ever begged for anything like that. Pauline bent over the table and gave her sister an awkward, spasmodic hug.

"There, there, Sister. I didn't know you would take it so hard. I'll let it stand till next fall. But won't you feel just the same about it then?"

Lucy lifted her face. "I won't be here then. I'll be off making my living, somewhere. I know you have to make up for Father's easy ways." She said this very low, and swallowed a lump in her throat. "But if you'll just — just humour me this year, you'll never be sorry. Some time you'll understand."

"All right, my dear. I'll go and send Poole away. And you go upstairs now and put your clothes on. Take this cup of coffee along, and drink it while you dress."

Lucy took it with gratitude, and went up the back stairs slowly, meekly, like a child who has been whipped until, as they say, its will is broken.

At the top of the stairs, before the door of his bedroom, stood a man who was also afraid of Pauline. He was freshly shaven, in a clean shirt, with bay rum on his greying hair and goatee. He took the coffee-cup from Lucy, put it on his dresser, and then took her in his arms. He kissed her with love, as he always did when he kissed her at all, on her lips and eyes and hair. He said not a word, but, keeping his arm around her, went with her to her own door, carrying the coffee.

3

As Lucy was coming in from the orchard just before sunset, she found Pauline waiting for her on the back porch, with a cape over her shoulders.

" Lucy, you'll take cold, you shouldn't be out there after four o'clock without a coat on. I never could make you wear clothes enough when you were little. It's just the same now. Mrs. Ramsay called up again and wants to speak to you. You will have to go there tonight."

Lucy said she supposed she must. There was only one thing she really liked to do in the evening. She and her father had been playing some sonatas of Mozart after he came home from the shop. He had a harsh tone on the violin, but he seemed to enjoy playing with her so much that she enjoyed it, too.

After supper she walked toward the town and turned into the street that people jokingly called Quality Street, because Mrs. Ramsay lived at one

end of it and the Gordons at the other. Mrs.
Ramsay was sitting in her high-backed chair beside the big front window, the shades up and
the silk curtains drawn back. This had always
been her way, though her house was so near the
sidewalk that every passer-by could gaze in; her
neighbours sometimes said it looked as if she
were giving a reception to the street. As a little
girl Lucy had loved to come to this house; such
comfortable rooms, old-fashioned furniture, and
soft, flowered carpets. She used to like the feeling that here there was a long distance between
the parlour and the kitchen, that they were not
always being mixed up together as they were at
home. Mrs. Ramsay was then the only woman in
town who kept two maids; now Mrs. Harry
Gordon kept a man and his wife, Pauline had told
her.

Lucy kissed Mrs. Ramsay's cheek and sat down
at her side, on the bamboo stool with the red
cushion where she used to sit when she was learning to crochet. Nothing ever changed in this house,
and there was something in the air of it that one
was glad to come back to. The house had some
reality, had colour and warmth, because the
woman who made it and ruled it had those things
in her nature.

"Lucy, dear, you aren't treating me as well as

you always used to. Have I grown too old for you, at last?"

Lucy murmured that she didn't like to visit her friends when she was dull and out of sorts. She had stayed in the city and worked all summer, and that didn't turn out very well. "When fall came, I was not good for anything. My teacher's wife packed my things for me — and I let her do it, think of that!"

Mrs. Ramsay patted her hand. So it wasn't that Lucy had displeased her teacher and been sent away, as some people said.

"Well, my dear, if you don't feel like talking, you might come in and play for me sometimes. I had the piano tuned as soon as I heard you were home. And there it stands. Madge never touches it."

Lucy brightened. "Would you like that? I think I would! We have only the old upright at home, you know. The one in father's shop is a little better, but it bothers me to have people coming in and out. I didn't use to mind it when I was a girl."

"A girl? Good gracious, what are you now, I'd like to know? No, you mustn't practise much while you are at home. You look tired, my dear, and you walk tired. You need a long rest in country air, and there's no air like the Platte valley. Denver's too high, and Chicago's too low. There are no autumns like ours, anywhere. The fall we spent in Scotland, I count lost out of my life. Mr. Ramsay would have it, and he got enough of it!"

Yes, Lucy said, she was glad to be at home. A whole year of the city had been too much.

"But it was a good year, wasn't it? You must have been enjoying your work, or you wouldn't have stayed. And I hope you had plenty of fun along with it. I don't like to see young people with talent take it too seriously. Life is short; gather roses while you may. I'm sure you gathered a few."

Lucy smiled indulgently. "A few."

"Make it as many as you can, Lucy. Nothing really matters but living. Get all you can out of it. I'm an old woman, and I know. Accomplishments are the ornaments of life, they come second. Sometimes people disappoint us, and sometimes we disappoint ourselves; but the thing is, to go right on living. You've hardly begun yet. Don't let a backward spring discourage you. There's a long summer before you, and everything rights itself in time."

Lucy sat wondering why it was she could not talk to her old friend. On her way down here tonight, she had been thinking she would ask Mrs. Ramsay to summon Harry Gordon to this very parlour some afternoon (no one refused any request of hers), to give her a chance to talk with him, and to be present at the interview. But now she found she couldn't do it. She rose with a sigh and went over to the piano.

She played for nearly an hour. She liked playing on this piano again; it was the only good one in town. Long ago she had supposed it must be one of the best in the world. Mrs. Ramsay sat straight in her high-backed chair, her elbow on the arm, her head resting lightly on the tips of her fingers.

Had Mrs. Ramsay turned and looked out of the window, she would have seen a man's tall figure go somewhat pompously by. (The blind was still up, and the interior of the lighted room was as clear to the passer-by as a stage setting when the theatre is dark.) At the corner he did not go straight north as his way led, but turned and walked west, along the sidewalk that bordered Mrs. Ramsay's flower garden and carriage-house. He had been seized by a fierce impulse to go straight to her front door and into the parlour, — he almost did it. Now he meant to walk round the block and look in on that scene again. But by the time he reached the west corner he had recovered himself, and he resumed his way north. It had only knocked him out of his course one block, his pride told him; that wasn't much of a knock!

Book II

In little towns, lives roll along so close to one another; loves and hates beat about, their wings almost touching. On the sidewalks along which everybody comes and goes, you must, if you walk abroad at all, at some time pass within a few inches of the man who cheated and betrayed you, or the woman you desire more than anything else in the world. Her skirt brushes against you. You say good-morning, and go on. It is a close shave. Out in the world the escapes are not so narrow.

4

Lucy returned from her call on Mrs. Ramsay in a cheerful mood and went to bed. At about four o'clock in the morning Pauline was awakened by a cry of fright in the next room, a cry of pleading and terror. Then there was a smothered whimpering that made her shiver. Once a puppy, run over by a wagon in front of their house, had cried like that.

It was not the first time Lucy had cried in her sleep. Usually she soon wakened, and then Pauline could hear her turning in bed and changing her pillows. She had never gone in to speak to her sister; she was afraid, really. There was something the matter with Lucy, no doubt of that, and Pauline was glad she had let the apple orchard alone. It must be good for her to be out there in the sun.

In her own way Pauline loved her sister, though there had been moments when she certainly hated her. Personal hatred and family affection are not incompatible; they often flourish and grow strong together. Everything that was most individual and characteristic in Lucy she resented; but she was loyal to whatever she thought was Gayheart. When someone praised Lucy's playing, Pauline usually said: " Oh, yes, all the Gayhearts are musical! If my voice had been cultivated . . ." Pauline was the soprano and director of the Lutheran choir.

Pauline was a much more complex person than her sister: her bustling, outright manner was not quite convincing, for all its vehemence. One felt that it had very little to do with her real feelings and opinions — whatever they might be. She was, so to speak, always walking behind herself. The plump, talkative little woman one met on the way to choir practice, or at afternoon teas, was a mannikin which Pauline pushed along before her; no one had ever seen the pusher behind that familiar figure, and no one knew what that second person was like. Indeed, Pauline told herself that she " put up a front." She thought it very neces-

sary to do so. Her father was queer, not at all like
the real business men of the town; and Lucy, certainly, was not like other people. Someone had to
be "normal" (a word Pauline used very often)
and keep up the family's standing in the com-
munity.

When Lucy was a child, Pauline was very fond
and proud of her, as if she were a personal
ornament reflecting credit on herself. She was
only eighteen when her mother's death left Lucy
entirely to her care. Friends and neighbours often
praised the way in which she brought the little
girl up. Pauline had loved looking after her, indeed, though she was often perplexed by the
child's wild bursts of temper and her trick of running away. It was not until Lucy was old enough
to go to high school that Pauline began to be
jealous of her. Then she realized that everyone,
even the Lutheran pastor and the Frau Pastor,
had one manner with her and another one with
Lucy. Mrs. Ramsay and Harry Gordon's mother
were always sending for Lucy on one pretext or
another. Pauline was asked to their houses only
when they gave a church supper, or a benefit for
the firemen. And Lucy's father spoiled her; that
was Pauline's sorest jealousy. If at breakfast she
told Lucy to come directly home after school and
help her with the ironing, Mr. Gayheart was

very apt to say that she must stop first at the shop and do her practising.

After months of brooding, Pauline went into her father's room one Sunday afternoon and told him she would like to have a talk with him. Was she to go on having all the care of the house, now that Lucy was old enough to share it? Was that fair to her, or good for Lucy?

Mr. Gayheart put down his newspaper and turned in his chair to face his daughter.

"It is more important that she does her music well and sits at the piano where I can watch her. If there is too much to do here, get one of Kohl-meyer's daughters to help you. You can get one for a dollar a day."

Pauline protested that it was not herself, but Lucy she was thinking of. Was it good for a girl to grow up heedless, and always to be waited on?

"I mean her to grow up at the piano. She will do more good there, and that is where she be-longs." Gayheart took up his paper again.

"The piano is in the parlour," Pauline said to herself, as she went back to her own room. "It has always been like that; the parlour cat and the kitchen cat."

Mr. Gayheart thought his elder daughter a girl of good common sense; she must see that

Lucy was different, everybody saw that; therefore she should make no fuss about it.

Harry Gordon was less obtuse. He knew that Pauline was jealous. Whenever he met her on the street, or when she came into the bank on business, he made a point of being cordial, and he always sent her a big box of candy at Christmas time. He seldom went to the house, however, even to see Lucy; merely called for her to take her for a drive or to a dance.

Pauline knew she would be quite as popular in the town as Lucy, if she were as pretty. Indeed, she was popular. People said: "Pauline is level-headed." Since that was the role she affected, she shouldn't have minded. But she did mind, very much. People were always stopping her on the street to ask when Lucy would be back from Chicago. The old ladies beamed at her with expectant eyes when they said how pretty Lucy was growing, as if Pauline should beam, too. She did her best, but a rather greenish, glow-worm gleam it was.

Lucy had never been aware of any of these hidden feelings in her sister. Her thoughts ran outward, and she was usually all aglow about something, if it were only the weather. She hadn't the least idea of what Pauline was really like — never considered it. Pauline had brought her up, taken care of her when she was sick, made birthday and Christmas parties for her. Pauline was "good," and good people were usually fussy and a little tiresome. Home, for some reason, was a place where she never felt entirely free, except in the orchard and the attic. Though Lucy would stoutly have denied such a charge, the truth was that Pauline's housekeeping was more pretentious than efficient. In spite of her bustling manner Pauline was really, like her father, very indolent.

Where there is one grievance, there are likely to be many. Pauline had never felt that her father could afford to send Lucy away to study. Lucy had earned nothing during her first two winters in Chicago. Mr. Gayheart paid for her lessons and her living expenses. That was why he was always short of money, and why Pauline had to raise onions. If Lucy had been apologetic and humble, and had practised small economies, she would have been less to blame in her sister's eyes. But not at all; she never seemed to think about money. When she had any, she spent it gaily. She refused to be poor in spirit. One expectation had enabled Pauline to put up with Lucy's easy ways and to endure this alarming drain on the family resources. The one thing Lucy could have done to repay her family for the "sacrifices" they had

made for her would have been to marry Harry
Gordon. Pauline had counted on that, and now it
had come to nothing — worse than nothing.
People were feeling sorry for the Gayhearts.
Pauline held her chin high, but her pride smarted
at the thought that Lucy had been jilted. She was
jealous of Lucy and for Lucy at the same time.

5

Lucy was going slowly along the street in the
centre of the town, approaching the Platte Valley
Bank. She had in her handbag a draft from Chicago, for the balance she had left on deposit
there. She had been carrying this draft about for
more than a week, passing and repassing the
bank in the hope of seeing Harry Gordon at the
cashier's window and surprising him before he
could retreat to his private office. This morning
she looked in once again as she went by; Milton
Chase, the young cashier, was at the window.
Lucy walked deliberately on to the end of the
main street, and went into the Union Pacific railway station.

After lingering about the waiting-room for a
while, reading the posters, she walked back to the
bank. There stood Harry in the cashier's cage.

It was bound to happen some time. She went in quickly, straight to the window.

" Good morning, Harry. Can I open a very small account with you while I am at home ? "

" Why, certainly! Milton," he called over his shoulder to his cashier, " a moment, please."

Milton came, and Harry stepped aside and motioned him to the window. Then he spoke directly to Milton, in his best business manner. "Miss Gayheart wants to open an account with us. Just fix her up with a pass-book. And I want you to give her your personal attention. Anything we can do to accommodate her, we'll be glad to do, you understand." With this he left the cage.

Lucy did not know what followed, except that she came out of the bank with a pass-book and a little cheque-book in her bag. So this, too, had failed.

She had thought if she could confront Harry at the window she would have courage to ask him to see her in his private office for a moment, and she would tell him — she did not know exactly what. Perhaps she would make him understand that she had told him a falsehood in the dining-room of the Auditorium that night. And she would ask him if he couldn't feel kindly toward her, for old times' sake, and speak kindly when they happened to meet. That was all she wanted, and it would mean a great deal to her.

And why, she wondered, as she walked home blindly, her eyes turned inward, would it mean so much? She didn't know. Perhaps it was an illusion, like the feeling she had in Chicago that if she once got home she wouldn't suffer so much. Perhaps it was because he was big and strong, and a little hard. He knew the world better than anyone else here, he had some imagination. He rose and fell, he was alive, he moved. He was not anchored, he was not lazy, he was not a sheep. Conceited and canny he was most days of the month; but on occasion something flashed out of him. There was a man underneath all those layers of caution; he wasn't tame at the core. If he should put his hand on her, or look directly into her eyes and flash the old signal, she believed it would waken something and start the machinery going to carry her along.

6

Crazy little Fairy Blair came home for Thanksgiving. On the very day she arrived she ran after Lucy on the street, in a grass-green cap and sweater.

"Hello, Lucy, wait a minute!" she called. Catching up with Lucy, she took her arm. "I'll walk along with you. I have a trade-last for you. One of my fraternity sisters has a brother studying with Professor Auerbach, Sidney Gilchrist, do you know him? He says Auerbach is crazy about you, and tells everyone you're his star pupil. Doesn't that please you? Oh, you're so haughty, always! And oh, Lucy! That Mr. Saint Sebastian who was drowned in Italy, wasn't he the singer you played for?"

Lucy had not heard that name spoken since she left Chicago. "Yes, he was." She could feel Fairy's sharp, mischievous little eyes.

"Terrible thing, wasn't it? Died trying to save a lame man, the paper said. Weren't you dreadfully upset? It must have been thrilling to play for him. Sidney said it put you in the upper circle all right!"

Fairy had heard that no one in town knew what was the matter with Lucy, and she thought she had a clew. That same afternoon she telephoned Pauline and asked her to come in for tea. (They called it tea, but it was always coffee and cake.) Fairy made haste to tell Pauline about the accident on Lake Como, and what Sidney Gilchrist had written his sister; that Lucy was desperately in love with Sebastian, and Professor Auerbach had been afraid she would go out of her mind.

Pauline went home very much relieved. Her sister had been here nearly three months, and this was the first hint she had got as to what had really happened. At least, it wasn't so bad as some people thought; the man hadn't jilted her. Pauline believed that to be jilted was almost the worst thing that could befall a respectable girl. Now she knew what to think of that moaning she sometimes heard at night; a shock like that would probably give one bad dreams.

She felt sorry for Lucy, — and a little in awe of her, for the first time in her life. Women like Pauline have a secret respect for romantic chapters. Lucy had been dignified, she reflected; she hadn't run about telling her troubles. She should, of course, have confided in her sister. She behaved strangely. Yet she, Pauline, would behave just so under similar circumstances; she was sure of it. Lucy was certainly a Gayheart.

When Pauline entered the house she greeted her sister in her usual cheery tone, but she was conscious of a certain awkwardness. Lucy was setting the table for supper, so Pauline came into the dining-room and sat down for a moment.

"Are you going to do anything special this evening?" she asked.

" I thought I might go down to play for Mrs. Ramsay. It's Saturday night, so Father will go back to the shop after supper."

" Lucy," Pauline began in a deeply confidential tone, " I don't know what we ought to do about Mrs. Harry Gordon."

" Do about her? Why, what do you mean?"

" She's never returned my call. I can't think why. Maybe she is waiting for you to call, before she returns mine. She coming here a bride, and we being old residents, perhaps she expects us all to come."

" Father too?"

" Now don't be contrary, Lucy! We who live here have to consider such things."

" Yes, yes, I know. But I shan't go to see her until she has been to see you. Let's let it rest at that."

7

As Lucy had been lost by a song, so she was very nearly saved by one. Two weeks before Christmas a travelling opera company, on their way to Denver to sing for the holiday season, gave a single performance in Haverford. Lucy had noticed the posters as she came and went about the town, but she hadn't even stopped to read them. One evening at the supper table her father took three blue tickets from his pocket.

"Girls, I think we must go to hear *The Bohemian Girl* next week."

From his manner Lucy could see that he was looking forward to this entertainment. He began asking her to tell him about the operas she had heard in Chicago. Pauline remarked that the " local talent " was to give *Pinafore* in February.

"That Gilbert and Sullivan stuff, I can't see much in it," said Mr. Gayheart. " If you want something light and amusing, now, there is *Die Fledermaus*. Or *La Belle Hélène*. You never heard it, Lucy? I was crazy about that opera when I was a boy. *The Bohemian Girl* is a little old-fashioned, maybe, but it's very nice."

On the evening of the performance Mr. Gayheart came home early. He took a bath and shaved very carefully, put on his best black suit, a white waistcoat, and his patent-leather shoes. When he came downstairs before supper, his daughters knew he expected to be admired.

"Do put on your new evening dress, Lucy. It will please him," Pauline whispered as they went to their rooms.

Lucy had meant never to wear that dress again, but she relented. Her father had so little to make him feel gay.

When they were getting ready to start, a light snow began to fall, and Mr. Gayheart was fearful for his patent leathers. He put his hand affectionately on Lucy's bare shoulder. " A little shawl or something, maybe, to carry along? I don't want you to take cold down there."

Lucy straightened his black necktie and slipped her arm around his neck for a moment, remembering the days in his shop when he used to keep his ear on her practising while he looked through a glass into the insides of watches.

Mr. Gayheart set off through the snow flurry, a daughter on either arm. He liked to reach the Opera House early and watch the people come in. (The theatre in every little Western town was then called an opera house.) On the way he told Lucy the manager of the house had put in folding chairs in place of the old straight-back wooden ones; otherwise she would find the hall just the same as when she played on the stage for her own commencement exercises, nearly four years ago.

When the conductor, who was also the pianist, appeared, Mr. Gayheart settled back with satisfaction, and the curtain rose on the hunting scene. The chorus was fair, the tenor had his good points; but before the first act was over, the three Gayhearts were greatly interested in the soprano. She was a fair-skinned woman, slender and grace-

ful, but far from young. She sang so well that Lucy
wondered how she had ever drifted into a little
road company like this one. Her voice was worn,
to be sure, like her face, and there was not much
physical sweetness left in it. But there was another
kind of sweetness; a sympathy, a tolerant understanding. She gave the old songs, even the most
hackneyed, their full value. When she sang: " I
dreamt that I dwelt in marble halls," she glided
delicately over the too regular stresses, and subtly
varied the rhythm. She gave freshness to the foolish old words because she phrased intelligently;
she was tender with their sentimentality, as if they
were pressed flowers which might fall apart if
roughly handled.

Why was it worth her while, Lucy wondered.
Singing this humdrum music to humdrum people,
why was it worth while? This poor little singer
had lost everything: youth, good looks, position,
the high notes of her voice. And yet she sang so
well! Lucy wanted to be up there on the stage with
her, helping her do it. A wild kind of excitement
flared up in her. She felt she must run away tonight, by any train, back to a world that strove
after excellence — the world out of which this
woman must have fallen.

It was long before Lucy got to sleep that night.
The wandering singer had struck something in her

that went on vibrating; something that was like
a purpose forming, and she could not stop it. When
she awoke in the morning, it was still there, beating like another heart. Day after day it kept up
in her. She could give her attention to other
things, but it was always there. She felt as if she
were standing on the edge of something, about to
take some plunge or departure.

8

The day before Christmas opened with a hard
snow-storm. When the Gayhearts looked out of
their windows the ground was already well covered, the porches and the hedge fence were drifted
white. At breakfast Mr. Gayheart said that when
he went down to make the furnace fire at six
o'clock, the snow must have been falling for some
time.

Lucy spent the morning tramping about in the
storm on errands for Pauline. She took boxes of
Christmas cakes to all their old friends, carried
a pudding in its mould out to the Lutheran pastor's
house at the north end of town, where there was
no sidewalk and she had to wade through deep
snowdrifts. The storm brought back the feeling
children have about Christmas, that it is a time of

miracles, when the angels are near the earth, and
any wayside weed may suddenly become a rose
bush or a Christmas tree.

Pauline was delighted to see Lucy so like herself
again. She invented errands to keep her going.
But late in the afternoon she thought her sister
looked tired, and sent her upstairs to her own
room to rest until supper time.

Lucy did not feel tired, she was throbbing with
excitement, and with the feeling of wonder in the
air. She put the blinds up high and sat down in a
rocking-chair to watch the bewildering, silent de-
scent of the snow, over all the neighbours' houses,
the trees and gardens. She was alone on the upper
floor. The daylight in her room grew greyer and
darker. Lights in the house across the street began
to shine softly through the storm. She tried to feel
at peace and to breathe more slowly, but every
nerve was quivering with a long-forgotten restless-
ness. How often she had run out on a spring morning, into the orchard, down the street, in pursuit
of something she could not see, but knew! It was
there, in the breeze, in the sun; it hid behind the
blooming apple boughs, raced before her through
the neighbours' gardens, but she could never
catch up with it. Clement Sebastian had made the
fugitive gleam an actual possession. With him
she had learned that those flashes of promise could

come true, that they could be the important
things in one's life. He had never told her so; he
was, in his own person, the door and the way to
that knowledge.

Tonight, through the soft twilight, everything
in her was reaching outward, straining forward.
She could think of nothing but crowded streets
with life streaming up and down, windows full of
roses and gardenias and violets—she wanted to
hold them all in her hands, to bury her face in
them. She wanted flowers and music and enchant-
ment and love, — all the things she had first
known with Sebastian. What did it mean, — that
she wanted to go on living again? How could she
go on, alone?

Suddenly something flashed into her mind, so
clear that it must have come from without, from
the breathless quiet. What if—what if Life itself were the sweetheart? It was like a lover waiting for her in distant cities—across the sea;
drawing her, enticing her, weaving a spell over
her. She opened the window softly and knelt down
beside it to breathe the cold air. She felt the snow-
flakes melt in her hair, on her hot cheeks. Oh, now
she knew! She must have it, she couldn't run away
from it. She must go back into the world and get
all she could of everything that had made him
what he was. Those splendours were still on earth,

to be sought after and fought for. In them she
would find him. *If with all your heart you truly
seek Him, you shall ever surely find Him.* He had
sung that for her in the beginning, when she first
went to him. Now she knew what it meant.

She crouched closer to the window and stretched
out her arms to the storm, to whatever might lie
behind it. Let it come! Let it all come back to her
again! Let it betray her and mock her and break
her heart, she must have it!

On Christmas Day Lucy wrote to Paul Auerbach to wish him a happy New Year, and to tell
him that she wanted to go back to him, if he had
any work for her to do. "I have found out that I
can't run away from my own feelings," she wrote.
"The only way for me, is to do the things I used
to do and to do them harder."

An answer came from him the following week;
a long, kind letter which must have taken most of
his Sunday morning. He and Mrs. Auerbach were
greatly relieved to hear that she felt this change.
The young man who had taken over Lucy's pupils
when she left so suddenly had been promised his
position until the first of April, when he was going
abroad to study. If Lucy would come on about
the middle of March, she could stay with them,
and Mrs. Auerbach would help her to find a room

and get comfortably settled before she went to work. "*You will have a warm welcome in the house of your old friend and teacher,*

Paul Auerbach."

Lucy had hoped she could go at once. Perhaps by March she would have lost her courage and be sunk in apathy again. But she could not ask her father for money, not with Pauline's narrow eyes always watching. She must look out for herself from now on, and she could do it. She must wait.

9

Lucy thought she ought to begin to study again, so she tried going to her father's shop every day and working on the sample piano. But Jacob Gayheart did not keep his ear open as he used to. He had gone backward in his music: he neglected it for chess. Soon after Christmas he had fallen away from playing duets with Lucy in the evening. He said he had to stay later at the shop, but his daughters knew that he was playing chess by telephone with a celebrated player who was visiting a cousin in North Platte. To be sure, he didn't often have a chance to match his skill with such an opponent.

Mr. Gayheart had let the shop get so dusty that

it wasn't a pleasant place to practise in. The space round the piano was full of broken music-stands and brass instruments that were never cleaned, and the walls were hung with dusty band uniforms. It embarrassed Lucy when people came in for watches and clocks that should have been repaired weeks ago.

If she stayed at home to practise, there were so many things to put her out. She was restless now, and trifles got on her nerves. No matter how orderly she managed to keep her own room, she couldn't help being aware that just on the other side of that thin partition her sister's room was in confusion. There was no doubting it, for Pauline left her door open. It was Pauline's custom not to make her bed until noon; she managed to get out of it in the morning without throwing off the blankets, leaving it like a mole-hill, with the very shape of her body.

"Lucy," she said one morning, "what's got into you, to be turning your mattress and sweeping your room every day? You never used to be so fussy."

"A little Italian showed me how a sleeping-room ought to be kept. I learned something besides music last winter," Lucy replied as she went downstairs.

Pauline squinted. That remark nettled her,

really hurt her feelings. She kept recalling it for days afterwards.

Lucy did what she could on the shop piano in the morning, and every afternoon she walked; through the town, and out the road to the north, where the land lay high and she could look down over the Platte valley. She began to notice things about the country that she had never taken much heed of before. She believed she was bidding the country good-bye this winter, and that made her eye more searching. One thing she watched for, every afternoon. Long before sunset an unaccountable pink glow appeared in the eastern sky, about half-way between the zenith and the horizon. It was not a cloud, it had not the depth of a reflection: it was thin and bright like the colour on a postcard. On sunny afternoons it was sure to be there, a pink rouge on the hard blue cheek of the sky. From her window she could watch this colour come above the tall, wide-spreading cottonwood trees of the town park, where her father led the band concerts in summer. Did that pink flush use to come there, in the days when she was running up and down these sidewalks, or was it a new habit the light had taken on?

If there was anyone in Haverford who could tell her, it would be Harry Gordon. He was the only man here who noticed such things, and he was deeply, though unwillingly, moved by them.

Book II

When she used to go duck-shooting with him she had found that he knew every tree and shrub and plant they ever came upon. Harry kept that side of himself well hidden. He could feel things without betraying himself, because he was so strong. If only she could have that strength behind her instead of against her! It was more than physical strength; it was something that could keep up to the bitter end, that could take hold and never let go. She was so without any such power that even to think of it heartened her a little. Perhaps some day they would be friends again. He was conceited and hard to teach, but she believed he would go on learning about life; because he had more depth than the people around him, and never pretended to like anything he didn't like. Quite the other way; he played at being a common fellow, and he wasn't. He was full of that energy which moves quietly, but always moves. It might get a man almost anywhere, she thought. And the people who hadn't it, even those with nice tastes, like her father, never got anywhere.

10

The weeks can be very long in the Platte valley, Lucy found. She began to feel trapped, shut up in a little town in winter. That long, soft, brooding

autumn had been like a kind companion. Now the
hard facts of country life were upon her. The
weather grew windy and bitter cold; the town and
all the country round were the colour of cement.
The tides that raced through the open world never
came here. There was never anything to make
one leap beyond oneself or to carry one away.
One's mind got stuffy, like the houses.

Toward the end of January came another heavy
snowfall; then a thaw, followed by a week of bit-
ing cold. The street, the roads, the yard, the orchard, were stretches of lumpy ice and frozen
snow. Why didn't Professor Auerbach send for
her now? If she could only walk past the Arts
Building once again, see the hall porter, and
George, the elevator man! If she could go to the
concert hall where she had first heard Sebastian;
sit in a corner, and remember! Some day she
would be able to rent his old studio, and she would
live there always. There must be ways of making
money in this world; she had never seriously tried,
but now she would.

One morning Pauline went to help the Metho-
dist women get the basement of the church ready
for a chicken-and-waffle supper, so Lucy practised
at home. She had found she could, if she were
alone in the house. At noon Pauline came in, resolutely cheerful (her sister was a hard person to

live with just now). When they sat down to lunch, she announced what she believed to be good news.

"Lucy, my dear, I've done pretty well for you this morning. I've got two piano pupils for you."

Lucy looked up and grew red.

"Pupils? I don't want any. I am not going to teach in Haverford."

Pauline didn't flush; she grew paler. "But seriously, Lucy, don't you think you ought to be doing something? You must know that Father gets deeper into debt all the time. We made a great sacrifice to send you away to study. I always supposed you'd want to pay back at least part of what it cost us."

"I will, some time. I can't see that anybody made a great sacrifice. It was Father's own idea that I should study music. I was never extravagant, certainly. I got along on less than most of the students."

Her careless tone made her sister indignant.

"More than sixteen hundred dollars you cost us in those first two years. I have the cheque stubs, and I know."

"So much as that?" Lucy asked in the same indifferent manner.

"That is a great deal, for us. You might have sent back just a little after you began to earn something, to show good intentions."

" I thought of it, but I bought clothes instead. When I was teaching I had to be decently dressed."

Both the sisters had stopped eating and both were making a pretence of drinking coffee. Pauline went on to say, as mildly as she could, that she had thought Lucy would like to take a few pupils, now that she was feeling better. " People here have always appreciated you. I wonder you haven't had applications before this. I'm afraid some of Fairy Blair's talk must have got around."

Lucy knew that she could go away and avoid a scene, but she didn't care.

" Just what do you mean? " she asked coldly.

The same thing happened to Pauline's face that happened to sour milk when she poured boiling water into it to make cottage cheese; it clabbered, the flesh curdled.

" The stories about you and that singer. Such things will get out, and Fairy isn't one to keep them. Now people are saying that when Harry Gordon went to Chicago last spring and saw how things were, he threw you over."

Lucy laughed disagreeably. " Threw me over, did he? Well, one story's as good as another. I don't care what they say. So you kept Father's cheque stubs, Pauline? How like you! You needn't

worry. I'm going back to teach under Auerbach
again. It's been arranged for weeks. The date is
set for March, but I can easily go sooner." She
had risen and was standing against the light of
the window.

Pauline broke out bitterly. " Lucy, why are you
so mean! Why do you hide things from us, and
treat us like strangers? "

" I suppose I feel that way," Lucy said as she
went up the back stairs.

While Pauline was washing the dishes she cried
a little, shed a few waxy tears that came hard.
You brought a child up, slaved for her and dressed
her prettily, did all the work and let her have all
the holidays (the parlour cat and the kitchen
cat!) — and this was what came of it. You cod-
dled her as if she were a superior being, and she
treated you like the housekeeper. And she used to
be so proud of her little sister!

When Pauline left the kitchen and came into
the sitting-room, she looked out of the window to
see who might be passing. Why, there was Lucy!
In her hat and coat, out of doors, out in the road,
hurrying away from the house and walking toward
the country. And she was carrying something, in a
black bag. Could it be her skating-shoes?

Pauline caught up a shawl and ran out into the
yard.

" Lucy ! " she called; then louder: " Lucy, wait ! "

But Lucy never turned. She seemed, indeed, to quicken her pace. Pauline went back into the house. " Just the way she used to run off when she was little ! " She dropped her shawl. " I wonder if she knows the old skating-place was ruined last spring when the river changed its bed? She'll have her walk for nothing."

Surely she wouldn't be crazy enough to try the ice out there? The bank had been torn up by the flood, and anyone could see that the river itself now flowed where the shallow arm used to be. Pauline considered telephoning the livery man to drive out after Lucy and tell her she wouldn't find any skating. But Lucy might be very much annoyed at any such interference. Probably it was the walk she wanted. Pauline remembered how she used to shut her eyes to Lucy's truancies; the child usually got over her tempers out on the highroad, but if she were shut up for a punishment it only made her worse.

II

Lucy found the walking bad enough. The roads had been rutted during the thaw, and afterwards the deep cuts made by the wagon-wheels had frozen hard. Yesterday's snowfall had packed into them. Her foot kept catching in the walls of the ruts. On either side of the wheel-tracks the mud had frozen in jagged ridges, rough and sharp like mushroom coral. Since yesterday few countrymen had been abroad, and the horses' hoofs had not yet broken down these frozen incrustations. Lucy couldn't remember that her feet had ever got so cold when she was walking; but this was not walking, really, it was plodding, and breaking through.

She was going west, directly against the wind, and she had often to turn and stand still to catch her breath. After she was a mile out of town, not a single sleigh or wagon passed her. It was still too early for the farmers who had gone to town in the morning to be driving homeward. The country looked very dreary, certainly. If only the sun would break through! But it made a mere glassy white spot in the low grey sky. In that cold light even the fresh snow looked grey, and the frozen weeds sticking up through it. In the draws, between the low hills, thickets of wild plum bushes were black against the drifts; they should have been thatched with yesterday's snow, but today's sharp wind had stripped them bare.

After the first mile Lucy began to feel very tired. The wind seemed to blow harder out here in the open country; it brought the tears to her eyes, and she had to keep wiping them away to see the road clearly. At last she determined to beg a ride from anyone who came by, even if he were going toward town. It was almost too cold to skate; and there would be the long walk home.

She had got over another mile when she heard the sound of sleigh-bells behind her. She turned her back to the wind, and listened. Only one man in the country had such bells. It must be Harry Gordon. There was no place to hide; she wouldn't hide. Perhaps this was the chance she had been hoping for. She stepped behind a telephone post and waited. She felt even colder than before, and her heart beat fast. She was afraid, after all. There he came in his cutter, over the brow of a hill, down into a draw where he was lost to sight, then out on the very hill upon which she was standing. She stepped into the middle of the road, in front of him, and held up her hand. He pulled in his horses and stopped.

" Harry, could you give me a lift as far as Thompson's pasture? I find it's pretty rough walking." She was standing with her back to the wind, her skirts blown forward, holding her muff against her cheek. She looked very slight and appealing out there all alone.

Harry's eyes were watery from the cold; he seemed more than ever to look at her through glasses. He began in that voice of cheery friendliness which meant nothing at all, with the usual shade of surprise in it:

"Well, now, I'm just awfully sorry, but I'm not going out that way at all! I turn north right here at the corner. I have an important appointment with a man up in Harlem. I'm nearly an hour late as it is, and I've got to make up time on the road. Wish I weren't in such a hurry." He touched his fur cap with his glove and drove on.

Lucy sent just one cry after him, angry and imperious, "Harry!" as if she had the right to call him back. His big shoulders never moved. His sharp-shod horses trotted on, the sleigh-bells singing, and turned north at the section corner a hundred yards away. The cutter with the upright seated figure moved along against the grey snow-drifted pasture land until at last it disappeared behind a group of distant straw stacks.

When Lucy next stopped to take breath, she found herself a long way nearer the river bend. For a moment she had leaned against the telephone post back yonder, but only for a moment. Such a storm of pain and anger boiled up in her that she felt strong enough to walk into the next county. Her blood was racing, and she was no longer conscious of the cold. She forgot to look where she put her feet; they took care of themselves.

She couldn't have imagined such rudeness, such

an insult! She was young, she was strong, she
would show them they couldn't crush her. She
would get away from these people who were cruel
and stupid — stupid as the frozen mud in the road.
If she let herself think, she would cry. She must
not give in to it, she must hurry on.

When she reached the river bank she sat down
just long enough to take off her walking-shoes, and
put on the other pair with skates attached. Her
hands trembled so that she could scarcely pull the
leather laces taut and tie them. She was angry with
herself, too. That she should have given him the
chance to leave her in the road, as he had left her
in the dining-room that night in Chicago! But how
could anyone be armed against such boorishness
and spite? Catching up a stick, she got to her feet
and took a few long strokes close to the shore. She
was not looking about her, she saw nothing —
she would get away from this frozen country and
these frozen people, go back to light and freedom
such as they could never know.

Without looking or thinking she struck toward
the centre for smoother ice. A soft, splitting sound
brought her to herself in a flash, and she saw dark
lines running in the ice about her. She turned
sharply, but the cracks ran ahead of her. A sheet
of ice broke loose and tipped, and she plunged to
her waist into cold water.

Lucy was more stimulated than frightened; she had got herself into a predicament, and she must keep her wits about her. The water couldn't be very deep. She still had both elbows on the ice; as soon as she touched bottom she could manage. (It never occurred to her that this was the river itself.) She was groping cautiously with her feet when she felt herself gripped from underneath. Her skate had caught in the fork of a submerged tree, half-buried in sand by the spring flood. The ice cake slipped from under her arms and let her down.

At half-past three, when the wind had grown so bitter, Pauline telephoned her father to drive out and pick Lucy up on the west road. Mr. Gayheart went to the livery barn a few doors from his shop and told Gullford, the driver, to put in two horses. Then he asked his friend the tailor to go with him for a sleigh-ride. Mr. Gayheart was not a man to look for trouble. But as they drove on and on and still did not meet his daughter, he grew uneasy.

When they reached the place on the shore from which the young people used to go skating, they found the ice out in the stream cracked and broken. So she couldn't have tarried here. She must have taken some other road, or gone to pay a call at one of the farms. The driver noticed something, out where the ice was bad; he said it looked like a red scarf.

Mr. Gayheart jumped out of the sleigh. He contradicted Gullford, but begged him to look again, to go out on the ice.

" I'm a little afraid to go out there, Mr. Gayheart; it's rotten. But don't get excited. Stay where you are, and I'll have a look around."

Gullford went slowly along the shore, considering what was to be done. He knew that was a scarf out there. Presently he stopped and bent over. Under a willow bush at the river's edge he found a pair of shoes and overshoes. He called Schneider, the tailor, and asked him to stay here with Mr. Gayheart while he whipped up his team and went to the neighbouring farms for help.

In less than an hour farm wagons and sleds were coming toward the river, bringing ropes, poles, lanterns, hay-rakes. One wagon brought a heavy row-boat that had been used in times of freshet. It was already dark, and the men who had come together agreed they could do nothing until morning. Mr. Gayheart kept begging them to try, declaring that he would not leave the river bank that night. While the older men talked and hesitated, four young lads dragged the old boat out into the rotten ice and groped below with their poles and hay-rakes. It did not take them a great while. The sunken tree that had caught Lucy's skate still held her there; she had not been swept on by the current.

When Harry Gordon and his singing sleigh-bells came over the hills from Harlem that night, he overtook a train of lanterns and wagons crawl-ing along the frozen land. In one of those wagons they were taking Lucy Gayheart home.

BOOK III

BOOK III

I

One winter afternoon, twenty-five years after Lucy Gayheart's death, the good people of Haverford met at the burying-ground for another funeral. Mr. Gayheart's body had been sent home from the hospital in Chicago where he had gone for an operation. It was four o'clock in the afternoon, an unusual hour for a funeral, but the hour had been determined by the arrival of the railway train. The coffin was taken from the express car to the Lutheran church in an automobile hearse (these are modern times, 1927), and after a short service it was brought to the graveyard.

Scarcely anyone could remember so large a funeral. Old Mr. Gayheart, as he had been called for years now, had many friends. Since Pauline's death, five years ago, he had gone on living in

his own house, with one of the tailor's daughters
as his housekeeper. He had kept his shop open,
and he continued to practise a little on his clarinet,
though he complained that his wind was failing
him. On Sundays, in summer, he sometimes practised out in the old orchard — which had never
been cut down.

He had lived a long and useful life, people were
thinking as they walked, or drove slowly in their
cars, out to the cemetery. Almost every timepiece
in Haverford was indebted to him for some attention. He was slow, to be sure, but to the end he was
a good workman. Last night, when they wound
their watches, many a one of his old customers
paused and wondered; tick, tick, the little thing in
his hand was measuring time as smartly as before,
and old Mr. Gayheart was out of the measurement
altogether.

By four o'clock the graveyard was black with
automobiles and people. The cars formed a half-
circle at some distance away, and their occupants,
except the old and feeble, got out and stood
around the open grave. The grey-haired business
men had once been "band boys." The young men
had taken lessons from Mr. Gayheart even after
he stopped leading the town band. His older pupils
looked serious and dejected; how many memories
of their youth went back to the music-teacher who

had lived so long, and lived happily, in spite of misfortunes!

It was sad, too, to see the last member of a family go out; to see a chapter closed, and a once familiar name on the way to be forgotten. There they were, the Gayhearts, in that little square of ground, the new grave standing open. Mr. Gayheart would lie between his long-dead wife and his daughter Lucy; the young people could not remember her at all. Pauline they remembered; she lay on Lucy's left. There were two little mounds in the lot; sons who died in childhood, it was said. And now the story was finished: no grandchildren, complete oblivion.

While the prayers were being read, someone whispered that it was almost as if Lucy's grave had been opened; the service brought back vividly that winter day long ago when she had been laid to rest here, so young, so lovely, and, everyone vaguely knew, so unhappy. It was like a bird being shot down when it rises in its morning flight toward the sun. The townspeople remembered that as the saddest funeral that had ever drawn old and young together in this cemetery.

By the time the grave was filled in and the flowers were heaped over it, the sun had set, and a low streak of red fire burned along the edge of the prairie. The crusted snow in the open fields

turned rose-colour. The automobiles began slowly
to back out, and the people who had come on foot
turned their steps homeward. In the company walking toward the town, one man withdrew from the
slow-moving crowd. Forsaking the road, he struck
off alone across a fenced pasture; a tall man of
solid frame, walking deliberately, his hands in the
pockets of his overcoat, his head erect, his shoulders straight. To a stranger he would have given
an impression of loneliness and strength — tried
and seasoned strength. He has need of it, for he
has much to bear.

2

Harry Gordon went directly from the cemetery
to his bank and called up his house by telephone.
The maid answered. Would she tell Mrs. Gordon
that he must finish up some business he had laid
aside to go to the funeral. He would have supper sent in from the hotel and would not be home
until late.

This done, he went through a hallway to his
private office. The first Gordon bank in Haverford was a wooden building. When the brick bank
was built, Harry's father had the old building
pushed back to the rear, and for years used it as a

storehouse. Harry, after his marriage, had fitted it up for a study and private office. At first it had looked like any country lawyer's office; oak tables, shelves that held old ledgers and financial reports. Gradually, almost stealthily, he had made it more comfortable, and as the years went on he spent more and more time there. The room was heated by the bank furnace, but he had put in a fireplace where he burned coke when the steam got low after banking hours.

This evening when he came in, Gordon lit a fire before he took off his overcoat. He unlocked a cupboard, got out his whisky and a siphon of soda, and sat down by the fire. Pouring himself a drink, he swallowed it slowly. Then he lit a cigar and with a long sigh settled deep into his chair. His well-set, vigorous frame relaxed. As he lay against the leather cushions he looked tired, — tired and beaten.

He had just buried the last close personal friend he had in the world. He was not, he thought with a grim smile, likely to make new ones at fifty-five. How differently life had turned out from the life young Harry Gordon planned in the days when he used to step out on the diamond to pitch his famous in-curve, with all the boys and girls calling to him from the bleachers!

For the last eight years he had played chess

with old Mr. Gayheart two or three evenings
every week. He had become a good chess-player,
quite Gayheart's equal. After Pauline's death left
the old man alone, Gordon managed to drop in at
his shop every day, if only for a moment. Chess
had become one of his fixed habits. They played
in Gayheart's shop, never at the house. They
talked no more than good chess-players usually
do. Gordon had watched games between players
of international renown when he was abroad during the war, and Mr. Gayheart liked to hear him
tell of them over and over.

Like many other men whose lives were dull or
empty, Harry Gordon " threw himself," as the
phrase went, enthusiastically into war work; Red
Cross, Food Conservation. Finally he went over
himself with an ambulance unit which he had
helped to finance. He was gone for eight months,
and his wife took his place as president of the bank
and manager of all his business interests. That was
probably the happiest period of her life; she was
a born woman of affairs.

For Gordon himself that absence did a great
deal; ever since he came back the townspeople had
felt a change in him. His friendship with old Mr.
Gayheart grew closer and warmer — like a son's
regard, indeed. At home he played his part better.
He and his wife seemed more companionable;

went out together, had guests to dinner. The air in their big, slippery-floored many-bathroomed house was not so chill as it used to be. And in business Gordon was more consistent. For some years before he went away he had brought on himself a reputation for eccentricity; this had gone so far as to affect his credit. At one time he would be sharp and tricky, barely keeping inside the law. At another he would let everything go, as if he felt a contempt for his business and were shuffling it off in the easiest way. Conservative men had begun to doubt his judgment.

Since his return from France he had devoted himself seriously to the bank, as his father had done, and he became more like his father. You knew where to find him now, Milton Chase said. There had been a stretch of time back there when Gordon's erratic decisions wore his cashier thin and bald.

Milton Chase probably knew more about his chief than anyone else did, but he didn't pretend to understand him. He had found it very agreeable to work under Mrs. Gordon. She was a reasonable woman. When he gave her the facts about any proposition that came up, he could pretty well tell in advance what she would think about it. But Harry had sprung too many surprises on him. On the surface there was perfect accord between Gor-

don and his cashier, but deep down Milton was
chafed by a secret distrust. What was he to think
when one of the most self-centred of men began
to give not only his time but his money to the Red
Cross? And worse was to follow. On the morning
when Harry called Milton into the room behind
the bank and told him that he was going to France
with the hospital unit, the cashier went to pieces
and said he didn't know whether he could face his
responsibility; he'd have to take a few days off
and think it over.

In the course of the years queer things had happened which Milton could never explain; things
which were out of order, which ought not to occur
in business. For instance, a shocking scene had
come about when they were foreclosing on Nick
Wakefield. Nick had been one of the gay young
fellows who used to play about with Lucy Gayheart. He inherited a big farm from his father,
but he was a town boy, didn't like heavy work,
and he failed as a farmer. When the bank was shut-
ting down on him, Nick nerved himself with plenty
of alcohol and came in to have it out with Harry
Gordon. The game was up, and he might as well
have his say. It was a very unseemly thing to occur
in a bank. Nick was full of bitter talk. He made
several ugly accusations, more or less true, and
ended with a taunt which brought the cold sweat

out on Milton's brow, as he sat trying to look small in his cage.

"You're ready to hit a man when he's down," Nick shouted, clenching his fists and standing up to Harry, " but you're a damned coward, for all your big chest. Afraid to go to poor Lucy Gayheart's funeral, weren't you, big man? Beat it for Denver! I guess there was a reason, all right!"

Milton had expected the ceiling to fall — he prayed that it might. But what happened was stranger. Gordon made figures on his desk pad for a moment. Then he turned in his chair and looked at Nick. He spoke to him in a voice that was really kind, without any contemptuous jollying in it:

"There are some names I wouldn't mention in your state of health, Nick. You're loaded, and you'll be sorry for this tomorrow. Come in then and finish what you have to say to me."

The bank sold Nick Wakefield out, but on terms more lenient than Milton Chase thought proper.

3

Harry had been sitting before the fire for nearly an hour when he switched on the lights and telephoned the hotel to send over some sandwiches. He dispatched them quickly and put the tray in the outer hall. Tonight was an occasion for remembering; he felt it coming on. Years ago he used to fight against reflection. But now he sometimes felt a melancholy pleasure in looking back over his life; he had begun to understand it a little better.

He, and he only, knew why he had been so brutal to Lucy Gayheart when she came home. It was not because of what she had told him that night after the opera in Chicago.

He had regretted his hasty marriage at the end of the first week; indeed, he was already regretting it when he made it. He knew that he was hurting himself in order to hurt someone else. He was doing the one thing he had sworn he never would do, marrying a plain woman, who could never feel the joy of life. Harriet Arkwright had her good points; she was not crude, she had some experience of the world. She was intelligent and executive. It was she who built their new house in Haverford, managed the builders and workmen without trouble or confusion, furnished it exactly as she wished — and paid for it. The house made a common interest, they were both pleased with it. She was reasonable, she had no irritating affectations. It would be possible to rub along, Harry thought. Then Lucy came back to town.

He knew, the first time he saw her in the post-office, that nothing had changed in him; more than ever before he knew what he wanted. She was standing in that crowd of slovenly men, clouds of tobacco smoke drifting about her, slowly turning the combination lock of her father's letter-box. As he stared in from the door the line of her figure made his heart stop. She looked so slight, so fine, so reserved — He had turned like a flash and walked rapidly down the street, without going inside to face her. But that glimpse of her, standing in profile with one hand lifted, had been enough.

Afterwards, from day to day, he had to see her at a distance, pass her on the street. That grace of person appeared more marked now, when she was withdrawn, than in the days when she had been careless and gay. She seemed gathered up and sustained by something that never let her drop into the common world. As she went about the town, her head a little bent, her glance veiled, she was sometimes spiritless and uncertain, as if she were beginning to walk abroad after a long illness; but she was unapproachable. That intense preoccupation, and her brooding look, were very sad to see in one so young. But they protected her, kept her aloof and alone. The boys she used to dance and picnic with were afraid to go to see her now. It was only when she met Harry Gordon that her eyes lighted up with the present moment, and

asked for something. They never looked at him
that they did not implore him to be kind.

He knew that she was unhappy, that she wanted
him to help her. Her voice had a note of pleading
if she but said good-morning — he gave her very
little chance to say more. She was a creature of impulse, he knew; never could conceal her feelings.
Perhaps she never tried. She made it clear that she
had some desperate need of him; it followed him
back to his desk after these chance meetings. Was
it that she had " got into trouble " as some people
whispered, and the man had deserted her? He
didn't know, he didn't care. He knew that if he
were alone with her for a moment and she held
out her hands to him with that look, he couldn't
punish her any more — and she deserved to be
punished.

He was in the first year of a barren marriage
(barren in every sense; his wife never had a
child), and the life he would have lived with Lucy
was always in the back of his mind then. She had
ruined all that for a caprice, a piece of mawkish
sentimentality. Let her suffer for it. God knew he
did! So he used to think, when he left her on a
street-corner looking after him.

And yet, underneath his resentment and his
determination to punish, there was a contrary con-

viction lying very deep, so deep that he held no communication with it. After they had both been punished enough, something would happen, how he didn't know; he might break with this town and all the guarantees of his future, but he and Lucy Gayheart would be together again.

A man who is young and strong looks forward. If he has been a fool and thwarted his own will — that is temporary. Every morning when he goes out into the air, he knows he is going to have his way; feels resourceful enough to leave all his blunders behind him. In those months after Lucy came back to Haverford, Harry had never doubted what the end would be. That would come about without contriving on his part — would come because it had to. When he passed her on the street or had to say good-morning to her in the post-office, the certainty of his ultimate mastery stirred in him like something alive. When the hour struck, nothing could stop him.

That evening when he passed Mrs. Ramsay's window and saw Lucy at the piano, and the old lady listening with her head resting on her finger-tips, he had scarcely got himself by. He had so nearly gone into that house. Then he would have walked home with Lucy, and everything would have come right.

Why was it that such terrible and unusual
things should happen to a prudent, level-headed
man? Why, when he came back from Harlem that
night, with miles of open country all about, did he
have to meet that little procession of lanterns and
wagons crawling along over the snow? Why had
he been compelled actually to drive in that procession? He couldn't pass it, — not after he had
stopped and asked what was the matter. He took
off his sleigh-bells and walked his horses into town
after the wagon train. There was nothing else to
do. — When he reached home he went directly
into the library, where his wife sat writing letters.
He shut the door behind him and asked her if she
knew what had happened at the river. Yes, Milton
Chase had called up to tell him as soon as the news
reached town, and she had answered the telephone.

" I am going west tonight on the Union Pacific
two-o'clock, and I will not be back until after the
funeral. I treated that girl very badly not long
ago. I've not said a kind word to her since she
came home. I can't go to the funeral; I'm not hyp-
ocrite enough. But I want you to go. The family
would be hurt if neither of us were there."

Mrs. Gordon frowned slightly. She was always
self-possessed, never made scenes. Then she said
in her cool, well-regulated voice:

" Your leaving town will be commented on,

probably? I can't see the point of my going to the funeral alone."

"It's the first favour I've ever asked of you."

"No need to put it in that way. I don't know the people, but if you think it's the proper thing to do, I'll go, of course."

"Thank you, Harriet." He went to his room to pack his bag.

There was not, in all the world, a living creature who knew of his last meeting with Lucy on the frozen country road beside the telephone post. For days, weeks, after his return from Denver, people talked about the "tragedy," as they called it; in the bank, on the street, wherever he went. He suspected they took care to discuss the subject before him. There was, of course, the dark whisper that it might have been suicide. The cuts on her wrists and hands showed that she had struggled to cling to the ice; but she might have lost courage after her plunge. She was last seen alive by a Swede farmer who had passed her on the west road, about a mile from town. Everyone knew she had been low-spirited and unlike herself since she came home. Fairy Blair had brought the story that some singer Lucy was in love with had been drowned in Italy in the summer; like enough she had resolved to put an end to herself in the same

way. Even if no one had happened to tell her that
the river had changed its bed last spring, couldn't
she see for herself? The whole west bank was torn
up, and the island was much farther from the
shore than it used to be.

These discussions never drew a remark from
Harry Gordon, and no one had quite the courage
to ask him how he happened to go to Denver the
night Lucy was brought home. " Let's see; you
met them on the road when they were bringing
her in, didn't you, Harry? " That was as far as the
boldest got.

Gordon put some more coke on the fire, walked
to the window, and stood looking up at the bright
winter stars. These things he had been remembering mattered very little when one looked up there
at eternity. And even on this earth, time had almost ceased to exist; the future had suddenly tele-
scoped out of the past, so that there was actually
no present. Kingdoms had gone down and the old
beliefs of men had been shattered since that day
when he refused Lucy Gayheart a courtesy he
wouldn't have refused to the most worthless old
loafer in town. The world in which he had been
cruel to her no longer existed.

Life would have been much easier for him, certainly, in those years after Lucy's death, if he could
have told someone about his last meeting with her.

Book III

Many a time, going home on winter nights, he had heard again that last cry on the wind—"Harry!" Indignation, amazement, authority, as if she wouldn't allow him to do anything so shameful.

Yes, he had had a long grilling. He was tough, but it had been a match for him. Luckily for him, the automobile had come along soon after the turn of the century. He owned the first car in the county, and, as they were improved, he bought one car after another. His farms were scattered far and wide, and he lived on the road. He often went to Denver for the week-end, "driving like the devil." He got into the habit of thinking aloud as he drove; talking, indeed, to his motor engine. Once when he had his wife along, he forgot himself and came out with: "Well, it's a life sentence."

That was the way he used to think about it. Lucy had suffered for a few hours, a few weeks at most. But with him it was there to stay. He understood well enough why she hadn't noticed the change in the river; he knew what pain and anger did to her. It was that very fire and blindness, that way of flashing with her whole self into one impulse, without foresight or sight at all, that had made her seem wonderful to him. When she caught fire, she went like an arrow, toward whatever end.

As time dragged on he had got used to that

dark place in his mind, as people get used to going through the world on a wooden leg. He made a great deal of money, he bought great tracts of land — rather a joke on him, now that land values were going down. But such things had kept him busy in the years when he needed distraction. His friendship with Mr. Gayheart had been a solace. It was somewhat like an act of retribution. Those evenings over the chess-board had come to be the best part of his week. He had grown to like the old man's shop better than any place in town. They never talked of Lucy, but the piano on which she used to practise still stood there.

Gordon was thinking, as he sat in his study on that night of Mr. Gayheart's funeral, how the sense of guilt he used to carry had gradually grown paler. For years he had tried never to think about Lucy at all. But for a long while now he had loved to remember her. Perhaps it was no great loss to have missed two-thirds of her life, if she had the best third, and had been young, — so heedlessly young. Of course she would fall in love with the first actor or singer she met, and would declare it openly. That would soon have passed. One might have foretold such adventures for Lucy, from her eyes, and from her laugh, — her low, rich, contralto laugh that fell softly back upon itself. It was not the laughter of nervous excitement; it was bubbling and warm, but there was a veiled note of recklessness in it.

In spite of all the misery he had been through on her account, Lucy was the best thing he had to remember. When he looked back into the past, there was just one face, one figure, that was mysteriously lovely. All the other men and women he had known were more or less like himself.

He sometimes thought of those mornings when she used to get up before daylight to go duck-shooting with him on the river: the heavy silence over the dew-drenched fields, the dark sound of the water, the quick flush of dawn in the east and the waking of the breeze in the tops of the cotton-woods, the birds rising in the pearl-coloured air. And at his elbow something eager, alert, happier than he could ever be.

It was a gift of nature, he supposed, to go wildly happy over trifling things — over nothing! It wasn't given to him — he wouldn't have chosen it; but he liked catching it from Lucy for a moment, feeling it flash by his ear. When they stood watching the sun break through, or waiting for the birds to rise, that expectancy beside him made all his nerves tingle, as if his shooting-clothes, and the hard case of muscle he lived in, were being sprayed by a wild spring shower. His own body grew marvellously free and light, and there was a snapping sparkle in his blood that made him set his teeth.

In the absolute stillness of the night (it was getting toward twelve), Gordon heard the bank telephone ringing again and again. That would be his wife, calling up to know what had become of him. He did not answer the telephone, but he covered the last glowing lumps of the coke fire, put on his overcoat, and started for home.

He is not a man haunted by remorse; all that he went through with long ago. He enjoys his prosperity and his good health. Lucy Gayheart is no longer a despairing little creature standing in the icy wind and lifting beseeching eyes to him. She is no longer near, beside his sleigh. She has receded to the far horizon line, along with all the fine things of youth, which do not change.

4

The day after Mr. Gayheart's funeral was Sunday. Harry and his cashier, Milton Chase, met at the bank by appointment, to go for a walk. People looked out of their windows to see them go by.

Everyone is used to the fact that Milton seems older than Harry. When his youthful good looks withered, they left his cheeks thin and his nose too long. He walks jerkily, with short uneven steps, as if he had left some unfinished business behind him. Harry still has the firm, deliberate tread with which he has come and gone about these streets for nearly a lifetime.

The two men are going "out to the Gayhearts'," as people still say. The town has not grown in these twenty-five years, it has shrunk. The old Gayheart place is still half-farm, lying at the extreme west edge of Haverford, where the sidewalk ends. Beyond, there is only country road. It is a walk Gordon often takes on a Sunday afternoon.

When he was a young lad, newly come to Haverford with his father, one summer evening he was riding out that road on his bicycle. The cement gang had been at work there all day, laying this very sidewalk which was never to go any farther. They had finished smoothing the wet slabs, stretched mason's cord on low stakes all about them as a warning to passers-by to keep off, and gone home for supper. When Harry came along on his wheel, he noticed a slip of a girl in boy's overalls, barefoot, running about the flower garden, watering it with a length of rubber hose. In-

stantly he recognized her as the same girl he had
seen in the skating-rink, gliding about to the music
in her red jersey. He got off his bicycle and walked,
pushing it beside him. She had not seen him. Suddenly she dropped the hose, glanced back at the
house to make sure no one was observing her, and
darted forward. She cleared the mason's cord and
ran over those wet slabs — one, two, three steps,
then out into the weeds beside the road, almost in
front of Harry. She looked up at him and laughed.

"Don't tell on me, please!" With that she
scampered up the dusty road and into the Gayheart yard by the driveway.

After all these years the three footprints were
still there in the sidewalk; the straight, slender
foot of a girl of thirteen, delicately and clearly
stamped in the grey-white composition. The travel
of the years had not made them fainter. To be
sure, there was never a great deal of walking out
this way; people came out here only when they
were going to see the Gayhearts. Gordon had never
heard anyone speak of these footprints; perhaps
no one knew who made them. They were light, in
very low relief; unless one were looking for them,
one might not notice them at all. The Gayheart
lots had not been well kept for a long while. In
summer the wild sunflowers grew up on either
side of the walk and hung over it; tufts of alfalfa,

escaped from the near-by pasture, encroached upon it, and a wild vetch with sprays of lavender-pink blossoms, like fingers, came up there every year and climbed the sunflower stalks, making a kind of wattle all along the two slabs marked by those swift impressions. For to Harry Gordon they did seem swift: the print of the toes was deeper than the heel; the heel was very faint, as if that part of the living foot had just grazed the surface of the pavement. Was there really some baffling suggestion of quick motion in those impressions, Gordon often wondered, or was it merely because he had seen them made, that to him they always had a look of swiftness, mischief, and lightness? As if the feet had tiny wings on them, like the herald Mercury.

Nothing else seemed to bring her back so vividly into the living world for a moment. Sometimes, when he paused there, he caught for a flash the very feel of her: an urge at his elbow, a breath on his cheek, a sudden lightness and freshness like a shower of spring raindrops.

Gordon and Milton Chase went over the Gayheart place thoroughly that Sunday afternoon, walked through the garden and the orchard, and the pasture beyond. The property now belonged to Gordon, mortgaged to him as surety for the loans the bank had made Mr. Gayheart during the last years of his life. If sold today, it would not bring a third of the amount the bank had advanced on it. Both men knew that. Gordon's plan was that Milton Chase should take the place over, and occupy the house rent-free, for life.

After they had tramped about through the dry weeds and dead grass, discussing what should be done with the orchard ground, and how the old barn could be made into a garage, they sat down on the porch steps and lit cigars.

"It's very generous of you, Harry," Milton Chase was saying, " but I'd much prefer that you sold it to me. I've lived in a rented house all my life, and now I'd like to own my own home," he ended plaintively.

" I'll call in Whitney tomorrow, Milton, and have him draw me a new will, leaving the place to you at my death, with no encumbrance. That will beat paying out good money."

Milton took off his hat and smoothed the thin hair about his ears with his hand. He didn't seem satisfied. He looked cold and tired and mournful.

Harry thought a moment and then said persuasively: "You see, Milton, if you bought the place and should die before me, your sons might sell it to — well, to anybody; to one of these retired farmers, who would make it into a chicken-yard. I'll never interfere with you; cut down the orchard, pull down the barn, do what you like. All I want is to retain a guardianship interest during my lifetime."

Milton still looked dejected, but Harry took it for granted that he had agreed to his proposition. "By the way, come over here with me a minute. There is just one thing I want you to see to." They walked across the lawn to the cement sidewalk. There Harry stopped. "This is a confidential matter, you understand, you'll not mention it. Those marks there in the cement were made by Gayheart's daughter Lucy, when she was a little girl. I'll just ask you to see that nothing happens to those two slabs of walk — in my time, at least." Gordon raised his voice a trifle and went on in a calculating tone, as if he were talking about alterations in a garage. "The cement seems firm enough. The only thing I can see that might injure it would be a wash-out. Heavy rains might carry the earth out from under one side, or a corner, and the blocks might tip and break. Keep an eye on them."

"I'll attend to it," Milton replied, just as he did to instructions given him at the bank.

Harry said he guessed he must go into the house now, to clear out the old man's private papers; he would see Milton at the bank in the morning. Milton walked slowly home. When he got there, he took a drink — a thing he seldom did. But he was cold; a little chilled and uncomfortable in his mind, too. He was unpleasantly reminded that there was, and always had been, something not quite regular about his chief; something fantastic, which he was secretly afraid of. That moment of conversation by the sidewalk had been very depressing, though he could not say just why. It had made him feel older; made life seem terribly short and not very — not very important.

Harry, with some amusement, watched his cashier's mournful back go down the street. He took a key out of his pocket and went into the silent, darkened house. He ran up the blinds in the living-room and let the four-o'clock afternoon sunlight pour in over the faded carpets and dusty furniture. Then he went upstairs. Mr. Gayheart had once mentioned (indeed the whole town knew it) that Pauline had always kept Lucy's room just as she left it when she went off to skate that day. After Pauline's death the old man kept the room locked, and let his housekeeper go in to sweep and dust only when he himself was standing by.

Gordon had all the keys. He took off his hat and opened the locked room. The shades were down, but they did not fit very well, and at the south window streaks of orange sunlight made a glow like candlelight in the dusky chamber. The closet door was kept open (prevention against moths), and dresses and dressing-gowns were hanging in a row. They had better be burned, he supposed. Beside her desk was a bookcase full of books and bound music scores; a chest in his private study at the bank would be the best place for those. He might look at them some time. Her toilet things were laid out on the dresser, and leaning against the mirror, in a tarnished silver frame, was a photograph of Clement Sebastian, with some writing on it, in German. This Gordon put in his pocket. It was the only thing he touched. He closed the door softly behind him, and locked it.

When he came out of the house the last intense light of the winter day was pouring over the town below him, and the bushy tree-tops and the church steeples gleamed like copper. After all, he was thinking, he would never go away from Haverford; he had been through too much here ever to quit the place for good. What was a man's " home town," anyway, but the place where he had had disappointments and had learned to bear them? As he was leaving the Gayhearts', he paused mechanically on the sidewalk, as he had done so many thousand times, to look at the three light footprints, running away.

WILLA CATHER (1873–1947) was born near Winchester, Virginia. When she was ten, her family moved from the peace of Virginia to the wild prairies of Nebraska. She was graduated from the University of Nebraska at twenty-one, and did newspaper work and teaching in Pittsburgh, Pennsylvania, for the next few years. She published a book of verse, *April Twilights,* in 1903, and a book of short stories, *The Troll Garden,* in 1905. They were followed, over the years, by twelve novels, including *Death Comes for the Archbishop, A Lost Lady* and *Shadows on the Rock;* four volumes of short stories, and two volumes of essays. Willa Cather was awarded the Pulitzer Prize for fiction in 1923.